Matthew Sánchez

Secret of the
SUNKEN SUB
Lee Roddy

PUBLISHING

Colorado Springs, Colorado

To all those special people who contributed so much during my research trip to Hawaii, including the following:

Howie Lindeman of Central Pacific Divers;

Lt. (jg) William J. Milne, Commanding Officer, USCGC *Cape Corwin* at Maalaea Bay, and Lt. (jg) Brad Nelson, USCG Public Affairs Officer, Honolulu;

Nat Padgett, skipper of the *Mala Kai*, and crewman Ermin;

Blaine Roberts, president of Lahaina Divers, Inc.;

Dennis De Rochemont, captain of the *Wailea Kai* catamaran, and the three crew members: Jim O'Brien, Chuck Martin and C. J. May;

Cliff Slater, president of Maui Divers of Hawaii, Ltd.;

Ninfa A. Tolentino, children's librarian, Maui Library District, Wailuku

SECRET OF THE SUNKEN SUB
Copyright © 1990 by Lee Roddy

Library of Congress Cataloging-in-Publication Data

Roddy, Lee, 1921-
    Secret of the sunken sub / Lee Roddy.
        p.   c.m.
    Summary: When twelve-year-old Josh witnesses the
sinking of a Soviet robot submarine off the coast of a
Hawaiian island, he becomes the quarry of Russian
spies racing to beat the United States Navy to the sub
and its secrets.
    ISBN 0-929608-63-1
    [1. Spies—Fiction.   2. Hawaii—Fiction.
    3. Submarines—Fiction.]   I. Title
PZ7.R6Sf   1990
[Fic.]—dc20   90-3155
                                               CIP
                                               AC

Published by Focus on the Family Publishing,
Colorado Springs, Colorado 80903
Distributed by Word Books, Dallas, Texas.

Editor: Janet Kobobel
Designer: Sherry Nicolai Russell
Cover Illustration: Ernest Norcia

Printed in the United States of America

96 / 10 9 8 7

CONTENTS

Pacific Ocean

Wailuku

Kahului

Lahaina

Olowalu

Maalaea

Auau Channel

Kihei

Maalaea Bay

MOLOKINI ISLAND

Kanahena

KAHOOLAWE

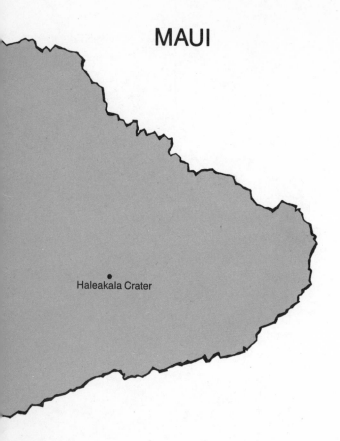

MAUI

Haleakala Crater

Chapter One

A MYSTERY AT SEA

J osh Ladd was standing with feet braced on the deck of the small fishing boat when he glimpsed something long and black below the surface. *Whale!* he thought, straining for a better look. *No, it can't be. But what is it?*

The boat slid sideways into a white-capped Pacific trough, cutting short the boy's view of the strange shape off the starboard* rail. He turned to the skipper at the wheel on the upper deck. "What's that?" he asked, pointing.

"Can't look just now, Josh," the deeply tanned captain replied without looking around. "I've got to concentrate on helping land that man's fish!"

Josh could hear his father and the half-dozen other passengers at the port* railing. They were shouting excited advice to a perspiring, bald-headed man fighting to

---

*The definition and pronunciation of words marked by an asterisk are contained in a glossary at the back of the book.

land a fish on a deep-sea rod and reel.

The twelve-year-old boy returned his gaze to the long, dark shape slipping silently through the open sea. *What in the world is it?* he asked himself.

Gripping the pitching rail with his left hand and hoisting his video camera with his right, Josh fixed his eyes on the dark shadow well below the two-foot ocean swells off Hawaii's shores.

Josh was a nice-looking boy with dark, wavy hair and well-developed upper body from years of swimming. In cutoff blue jeans, white tee shirt and basketball shoes, he closed his left eye and eased the right one against the camera's viewfinder.

Maybe it is *a whale,* he thought, *although Dad said it's too late in the season for them to still be here.* But Josh had brought his video camera along anyway in hopes of seeing one of the great mammals. They came annually to breed and bear their young in these waters off the island of Maui.* Josh pressed the "on" button and saw the red light wink on at the bottom of the viewfinder. He tracked the shadowy, gliding, underwater object as it headed out to sea.

Hawaii's waters are so clear that it's possible to see a hundred feet straight down. However, bright sunlight reflected from the surface in shimmering, silver sheets and prevented an unobstructed view of the object below.

While the camera whirred softly, recording both sight and sound, Josh felt a sudden rush of excitement as he thought, *If it's not a whale, what is it?*

The dark object seemed to be tilted slightly upward, as though it were trying to surface. Josh leaned far over the rail to see better. Suddenly, the long object shuddered and stopped. Very slowly, it drifted downward until it vanished into the ocean's depths.

Josh switched off the camera and lowered it to his side. He let his gaze sweep the ocean's vast emptiness, stretching to the horizon. There was no other vessel in sight. Slowly, he turned to look toward the Maui shoreline. Maalaea Bay* was almost straight ahead. To the right and closer to Josh, the ancient cinder cone called Kanahena Point* rose from the land. To the left were one large island and a tiny one.

The larger, standing well out to sea, looking somewhat like a miles-long whale with a square nose, was Kahoolawe,* the U.S. Navy's bombing range. It was about a dozen miles off the southern coast of Maui. The other island, farther in toward land, was called Molokini.* It was actually the tip of an extinct volcano that rose from the ocean's floor.

Josh looked again under the sea where the strange, dark shadow had disappeared. On an impulse, he pulled his Boy Scout compass from his pocket and quickly noted the location by taking bearings on Kanahena Point, Kahoolawe and Molokini. Since he didn't have pen or paper with him, he repeated the coordinates to himself several times until he had committed them to memory.

Then the boy turned to call out to his father about what he had seen. Before Josh could speak, however, his father let out a happy shout from the far rail, beyond the wheelhouse.

"Strike! Something's hit my bait, too!"

"It's a big one!" Josh cried, watching his father brace against the fish's run. "Look at the way he's taking your line!"

In the excitement, Josh momentarily forgot about the strange shadow he'd videotaped. He scrambled up onto the wheelhouse with his camera. The captain had allowed him to ride there on the hour-long trip from Maui to the fishing grounds.

"I'll get some footage, Dad!" Josh yelled, bracing himself once again. "Don't lose him before I get focused!"

Josh had shot considerable footage by the time John Ladd landed a fair-sized yellowtail tuna. As the boy and the other fishermen gathered around to admire the catch, Josh remembered the mysterious object he had glimpsed. But he didn't get to discuss it with his father because other fishermen began getting strikes. The excitement remained high on the trip back to harbor as four fishermen at the stern* continued catching fish almost to the breakwater* at Maalaea Bay.

Josh's best friend was waiting on the wharf when the boat docked in the town of Maalaea shortly after one o'clock. Tank Catlett was Josh's age but the exact opposite in temperament. He was slow and easygoing, while Josh was energetic. (Josh had been compared to a bottle of hot soda pop when someone yanks the cap off fast.)

Tank was blond, fair and slightly heavier and taller than Josh. Tank's nose always seemed to be sunburned and peeling. Like Josh, he was well developed in the shoulders, arms, back and chest from swimming.

"Catch anything?" Tank asked, looking at the boat tied up at the wharf. None of the men had disembarked yet, as they were taking snapshots of their catches now that the boat's pitching and rolling had stopped.

"I didn't fish, but Dad caught a twenty-two-pounder," Josh answered. He partially lifted the video camera. "I got some great shots of him landing it. I also got footage of something strange. Want to come up to the condo and see?"

Tank nodded, so Josh turned to call to his father, "Dad, I'll meet you back at the condo!"

Physically, John Ladd was a mature, taller version of his son. And both had a tendency to speak and move quickly. Mr. Ladd shouted back, "Okay, Son, but don't tell your mother about my fish. I'd like to surprise her."

Josh nodded and turned to walk away from the wharf with Tank toward a narrow, paved road. On the right, rows of multistory, concrete block condominiums were lined up along the big, open bay. On the left, acres of sugarcane stopped at a windbreak of be-still* and ironwood* trees that barely softened the stiff, northerly trade winds. The trades were usually gentle, but these fairly whistled from being funneled between the West Maui Mountains and the start of the massive bulk of a dormant volcano called Haleakala.*

Josh started to describe the strange sight he'd seen when a boy he didn't know stepped out from under one of the ironwood trees. He was about thirteen, an inch or two taller than Josh, with the look and movements of an athlete.

"Hey!" the newcomer said, grinning to show wide, even teeth from a dark-complected face. "You must be Josh Ladd and Tank Catlett! I was talking to your sisters, Tiffany and Marsha, and they told me about you two guys. Best friends since you were little, I hear."

"Still are," Josh said, setting the video camera on the pavement. "I'm Josh. He's Tank."

"I'm Ted Langford, but people mostly call me Macho."

Josh raised a questioning eyebrow. He'd heard the word *macho* often enough in Los Angeles, where his family had lived before moving to Hawaii. It was used to describe young guys who considered themselves more manly than others. If this new boy called himself Macho, it suggested an attitude Josh didn't like, and he didn't even know him yet.

When the boys had exchanged cautious hi's, Macho glanced down at the video camera. "Whatcha got?" he asked. "Video shots of whale watching?"

"Too late in the season for whales, I guess," Josh said.

"I thought I saw one, but I'm not sure. But I did get some footage of my father landing a fish."

"Yeah, we're just on our way to his condo to watch it," Tank added.

"Can I come along?" Macho asked.

Josh wasn't sure he wanted to befriend this stranger who might have an inflated ego. But he quickly decided there was no polite way to refuse, so he said, "Sure, why not?"

As the boys rode the elevator to the fourth-floor, furnished condo Josh's parents had rented for two weeks, Josh and Tank learned a little about Macho. Like them, he had been reared in Los Angeles. He and his parents now lived in a condo in the building next door.

Josh and Tank explained that their families had rented side-by-side condos for vacations. Afterward, they'd all return to Honolulu, where they lived.

At the front door of the Ladd condo, Josh automatically started to remove his shoes.

Macho chuckled and said, "I see you've adopted the Oriental custom of not wearing shoes in the house."

Josh retied his shoes self-consciously as he answered, "In Honolulu, Mom's got a white rug, so she makes us take off our shoes and leave them outside the door the way most of the local people do."

"I don't intend to give in to that stuff," Macho replied, following Josh into the condo. "I'm my own man. That's one reason they call me Macho."

Josh felt a tinge of annoyance and glanced at Tank. His

face showed he didn't much like this brash new kid, either. Josh thought, *He's new. We'll give him a chance to mellow out.* Then he raised his voice and called, "Mom, I'm home!"

There was no answer. Josh called again, "Tiffany? Nathan?"

When there was still no answer, he removed the cassette from the camera and set both in the hallway. He walked into the kitchen on his right, where his mother always left a note under a small magnet on the refrigerator door when she went out. Josh read aloud, "We've all gone for a walk on the beach. Back soon. Love, Mom."

Macho dropped so heavily into a rattan* occasional chair that Josh heard the noise all the way in the kitchen. "Hey, Ted," he cautioned, "take it easy on the furniture."

"Call me Macho," came the reply. The new boy added at once, "What've you got to eat?"

Josh turned in surprise. He and Tank always made themselves welcome at the refrigerator in either family's home, but it was jolting to hear a total stranger take such liberty as to ask for something the minute he came in the door.

Josh opened the refrigerator, thinking, *I know I'm not going to like this guy much.*

Tank appeared quietly at Josh's side. The blond boy lowered his voice as he said, "You ever see such nerve?"

Josh hesitated, fighting the feeling of resentment toward Macho. It wasn't in Josh's nature to make snap decisions against somebody, but it was hard to keep from feeling annoyed with Macho.

Josh handed three soft drinks to Tank and closed the refrigerator. As he reached into the cupboard for some crackers, he heard the videocassette recorder click on.

"Hey!" Josh called without thinking. "What're you doing?"

"Cueing up your cassette," Macho said.

Josh slammed the cupboard door and said, "I'll show the tape in a minute!"

"I've already got it running," Macho answered, turning up the volume. "Hey! What's that?"

Josh rushed into the living room carrying the box of crackers. His eyes fastened on the television above the VCR. The long, dark shape he'd photographed that morning loomed ominously on the screen.

Tank stopped beside Josh, holding the cold cans of soda in his upturned palms. "Yeah," he said, "what is that? A whale?"

"No!" Macho exclaimed, leaping up and taking a step closer to the screen. "It's a submarine! See it? That's a sub!"

Josh asked with rising excitement, "You sure?"

"I'll rewind it and play it again," Macho said. "Then I'll stop the tape and you can see for yourself!"

A moment later, with the dark object frozen on the screen, Macho's voice rose sharply. "I tell you that's a sub. Maybe the one that sank!"

"A sub sank?" Josh asked in surprise.

"Yes! There was a news flash a while ago from one of the Honolulu stations!"

Josh felt his blood warm in excitement. "What'd they say?"

Macho shrugged. "Just that the Navy's listening devices offshore had detected an explosion in a submarine. They think it sank."

"When? Where?"

"The Navy wouldn't say, except it happened this morning someplace off the coast of Maui."

Josh felt a sickening sensation in his stomach. "If it was a sub that sank, there may be men trapped inside—alive!"

Macho shook his head. "No, the newscaster said the authorities believe it was a smaller, remote-controlled robot. There were no people in it. Look! There's no conning tower,* which would be needed if it were manned. This *must* be the sub they were talking about."

"I've heard of two-man midget submarines," Josh said doubtfully, "but never a robot one."

"Well, you're seeing one now!" Macho replied. "My old man works for the government, so I hear things. I also know that if it had been one of our subs, there'd have been news about starting a salvage effort. Since there was no such announcement, that means the Navy must know it's another country's sub."

"Which country?" Josh asked.

"The Soviet Union," Macho said as if he were condescending to explain something obvious. "Hmm. Hey! I just thought of something!"

"What?" Tank asked.

"I mentioned that the Navy has different devices buried under the sea that can catch any sound like submarines sneaking around. By using two or three of those devices, the Navy can pinpoint pretty closely where the sub is. Of course, if it lost power and drifted some without making any noise before it sank, they might know only the general location. Still—"

"So?" Tank interrupted.

"So our country probably has a better idea where that sub sank than the Soviets do. They don't have any such listening devices around the islands."

"I still don't understand," Tank said.

Macho rolled his eyes impatiently. "It's obvious! Our guys will quietly go after the sub to try recovering its secrets. For example, the guidance system—how is it controlled? Then our guys would want to know what kind of weapons it carries! So the Soviets will want to get there first and keep our guys from learning. They'll be desperate to find the sub before our navy does. It's going to be a race!"

Josh felt his lips go dry as he thought of what Macho was saying. "I—I know where the sub is," Josh admitted. "I used my compass to take bearings at the spot where I saw it go down."

"Wow!" Macho said. "You know, the Soviets don't have a chance of getting to the sub first unless they get information about where it sank, and fast! They also don't want to have to admit they had a sub in Hawaiian waters, so they'll try to destroy any evidence of the sub's presence here. That makes you and your tape invaluable to them, Josh!"

"They don't know about me!"

"No, but if they find out you know where the sub is and you've got the tape, they'll do anything to get you!"

Josh felt a sudden sense of alarm. He sat down slowly on the sofa. After a minute he said, "Nobody knows but you two and me."

"I won't tell anybody, Josh!" Tank said.

Josh glanced at Macho and asked, "What about you?"

"Oh, you have my word! But I wouldn't count on the Soviets' not finding out. Since you're the only one who knows for sure where the sub is, you can bet they'll find out sooner or later. Then they'll come after you."

Josh sighed softly and licked his lips. Macho frowned and added, "You know, Josh, when that happens, I wouldn't give much for your chances! You're really in terrible danger!"

Chapter Two

TIGER
SHARK!

osh stared in startled surprise at the taller boy, then managed a nervous laugh. Turning more serious, he warned, "Don't try to scare me, Ted!"

"Macho," the older boy corrected firmly, "call me Macho. And I'm not kidding! If the Soviets ever find out you know where their sub sank—and you've got pictures—they'll do anything to get you to tell! So you really are in big trouble."

"I don't know anything about spies except what I've seen on television stories," Tank said. "But what Ted— uh, Macho—says sounds logical."

Macho added thoughtfully, "That sunken sub's got to be filled with Soviet secrets they'll want to keep from our navy, so they'll have spies everywhere. If they find out what you know, Josh, they'll have to make you tell where it is!"

"Maybe we'd better just forget keeping it a secret," Josh said. "I'll tell my parents, and they'll—"

"No!" Macho interrupted. "The last thing you want to

do is tell your parents!"

"Oh?" Josh asked, taken aback by Macho's strong tone of conviction. "Why?"

"Since our navy almost certainly has some idea where the sub is already because of its listening devices, there's no need to rush the video to the authorities. Better to keep what you know a secret for a while. But you know how parents are. If they find out, they'll figure they should go to the authorities right away with the tape and information—somebody like the FBI, CIA or some other federal agency. And maybe a Soviet spy has infiltrated one of those agencies, in which case they'll come right after you and your family!"

"There couldn't be foreign spies inside our own agencies!" Josh protested.

Macho snorted and said, "My father says a spy's not someone you find hiding under a bed, but a nice-seeming person who sits down to the dinner table with you."

"What's the CIA?" Tank asked.

Macho explained, "The Central Intelligence Agency. It was established by the National Security Act to handle all sources of our government's intelligence—you know, spy activities."

"Our government doesn't have spies," Tank argued.

Macho rolled his eyes upward again. "Boy, are you naive! Every country has spies, only it's called 'intelligence' because it sounds better. *Intelligence* means gathering or distributing information, mostly secret things about a possible enemy. And the CIA's job is to keep our government informed of what other nations are doing that might hurt us—including the Soviets!

"The FBI—Federal Bureau of Investigation—investigates violations of federal law and handles counterintelligence inside the country. The CIA's supposed to deal with things outside the country because every nation has spies working undercover.* Why, there might even be one in these condos!"

Josh spoke up. "Why would there be a spy in these condos? They're mostly filled with tourists!"

"Can you think of a better cover?" Macho challenged. "Hawaii's a mighty important military center right in the middle of the Pacific Ocean!"

Tank frowned, musing, "There are Navy and Air Force bases on Honolulu, plus the Coast Guard. In fact, there's a Coast Guard station here, and naval ships anchor at Lahaina.*"

"Right!" Macho exclaimed. "Lahaina's only fifteen miles away! I remember my father telling me about a Soviet ship that anchored right off Olowalu Point.* That's between here and Lahaina!"

Josh shook his head. "I just don't believe spies could be right here."

"What about Igor Petrov?" Tank said softly.

Josh turned to frown at his friend. "Just because he lives next door and has a Russian accent—"

"He told me once he was born in Russia," Tank

interrupted.

"That doesn't make him a spy!" Josh protested.

"Maybe he's not," Macho agreed, "but you can see what I say makes sense, can't you?"

Tank snapped his fingers as he said, "Josh, why don't you just erase the part of the videotape that shows the sub?"

"I thought of that, but I can't. After the sub, I shot footage of a fish Dad caught, so he's going to want to see that. There's no way I could explain why the first part of the tape was blank."

Macho suggested, "Besides, if we can figure out a way to get the tape to our navy without having spies there intercept it, they'd probably be able to learn something about the sub from watching it. Say, I could take the tape so you could say you didn't have it! That'd give us time to think about what we should do next."

Josh thought for a moment. "Okay," he said reluctantly, feeling a little guilty. He handed the cassette to Macho. "But I don't really like doing this. Remember, you both promised not to tell anybody."

That evening, Josh sat down to dinner feeling uneasy even though there was nobody present except his own family. After his father asked the blessing, the boy glanced around the table.

John Ladd was a nice-looking, six-foot-tall man. He had taught history in Los Angeles public schools until recently. Then he'd bought a Honolulu tourist publication and moved his family to the islands. His wife, Mary, was a tall, slender woman with very black hair and a dimple in her left cheek.

Tiffany, Josh's fourteen-year-old sister, was on one of her diets again. She picked at her food, although she was already slender and quite tall. She had short, brunette hair and bore a clear resemblance to her pretty mother.

Nathan, the ten-year-old youngest member of the family, had been the smallest boy in his California school class. He hadn't grown much since moving to Hawaii.

Josh's father finished swallowing a piece of broiled fish and looked across at his older son. "When're you going to show the video you shot of my landing that tuna?" he asked.

Josh squirmed and passed the fresh vegetable plate his mother had handed him. "Uh, I don't have it right now," he answered. "I loaned it to a new kid I met."

Tiffany was instantly the suspicious older sister who sometimes made life difficult for her brother. "How come?" she asked.

Josh shot her an irritated look. "Because he's a new kid and he asked to borrow it," he said a little too loudly. He tried to tell himself that was the truth, but his conscience bothered him. His parents had always said there was no such thing as a little white lie.

"Bet you really are hiding something, Josh," Nathan said. "What'd you do wrong?"

"Nothing!" Josh snapped.

Mary Ladd said reprovingly, "Now, Josh, there's no need to be so harsh with your brother. What's this new boy's name?"

"Ted Langford, but he calls himself Macho."

"Macho?" Nathan broke into laughter. "You've got to be kidding!"

"That's enough, Nathan," his father said quietly. He turned to Josh and asked, "You know we like to meet all your friends, so when can we meet this new boy?"

"I don't know, Dad."

"What does his father do?"

"Works for the government. The family lives in a condo here, but his mother's gone a lot."

There was a long silence, and Josh knew his parents were considering the information. Finally his mother suggested, "John, why don't you just tell us about your fish and we'll see the video some other time?"

Josh was glad to be off the hook for the moment. But he had an uneasy feeling he was starting to make a tiny snowball that could grow into an avalanche of trouble.

That evening the family donned bathing suits and went downstairs to the fenced-in swimming pool. Between it and the start of Maalaea Bay* was a small barbecue pit with two grills. One side was in use. The other had white ashes, showing someone had finished barbecuing and gone back inside the condos.

Josh recognized Igor Petrov tending fresh fish steaks on the nearer grill. Josh excused himself from his family and walked around the iron fence. "Hi," he said, feeling his mouth go dry, wondering if it was really possible this friendly looking, middle-aged man could be a spy. "What're you fixing?"

"Fresh ahi,*" the reddish-haired man replied in a raspy voice that held a strong Russian accent. He tapped the fish with a pair of stainless steel tongs. "Vat you call yellowtail tuna."

"My father caught one today," Josh said, trying to sound casual yet wanting to know more about this man. "About twenty pounds."

"More dan dat, dis!" Igor tapped the sizzling fish on the grill. "Sell part to store! One man like me can't eat so much, da?"

"Da?" Josh repeated.

"Means yes in old country." Igor smiled down at the boy. The man's hazel eyes were as friendly as his grin. "Mother Russia."

Josh had to swallow twice before he could sound casual asking his next question. "You're not a citizen of the U.S.A.?"

"Not yet, but some day!" Igor reached for a white platter resting on the side of the grill. "Dis ready, I t'ink. You vant come my place, have some?"

"Uh, no, thanks," Josh answered, watching Igor deftly lift the two fish steaks onto the platter. "How long've you been in this country?"

"Two years. Ve talk again sometime, da?" Igor smiled

and began scraping the grill vigorously with a wire brush.

"Yeah," Josh said, feeling as if he were being dismissed. He turned and walked around the iron fence by the pool, his thoughts whirling. *So he's not an American citizen; he's a Russian. But if he's a spy, why would he be so open about his background? Unless that's a way to make people think he really isn't a spy because it'd be too obvious.*

Nathan, sitting on a plastic-webbed chair inside the pool fence, asked, "What're you mumbling about, Josh?"

"Huh?" Josh was startled. He hadn't realized he'd been thinking aloud. "Oh, uh, nothing."

Josh walked down to the end of the fence and reached over the top to unlock the gate. He watched Igor disappear into the first-floor walkway in the adjacent building of condominiums.

Well, anyway, Josh told himself, making sure he didn't mumble aloud, *whether he is or isn't an agent, there's no way Igor could know about what I saw. Unless Tank or Macho told, and they swore they wouldn't.*

Feeling a little relieved but still concerned, Josh dived into the lighted pool with his father, mother and sister. He rolled over and looked up at the coconut palms rustling in the strong trade winds. As he floated on his back, he tried to think through the problem that had struck him so unexpectedly that day.

Tank wouldn't give my secret away, unless it slipped out, he concluded. *But I'm not so sure I can trust*

Macho. I've got to stick close to him so I can keep an eye on him.

After breakfast the following morning, Josh walked next door to the Catletts' condo. He was surprised to see Tank and Macho coming out the door wearing bathing suits and carrying snorkeling* equipment with flippers. Macho also had a sling gun* for spearing fish.

"Hey, Josh," Tank said, "want to go snorkeling with us? Oh, and guess what? Macho's got his Junior Open Water Diver Certification card, same as us!"

"You like scuba diving?*" Josh asked.

"Love it!" Macho answered, swinging the sling gun. "One of the first dives I'm going to make is down to that old World War II submarine the Navy deliberately sank in Lahaina Harbor a few years ago. A hundred thirty-five feet down! I'll bet when the Navy sank the *Bluegill*, they never dreamed that ordinary guys like us could someday dive that deep."

"Careful with that sling gun!" Josh cautioned. Then he added, "I read about the *Bluegill*. There's talk the Navy is going to raise it because it's become what my father calls 'an attractive nuisance.' "

Macho lowered the sling tip. "That's why I'm going to make it one of my first dives. You guys want to come along?"

Tank shook his head. "Josh and I are going to tackle something easier at first. Right, Josh?"

Ordinarily, Josh would have agreed with his friend. But

now he was most concerned about staying close to Macho to make sure he didn't reveal the secret. So, hoping to solidify his friendship with the older boy, he said, "Maybe we should try the sub."

Tank looked at Josh in surprise, but before he could answer, Macho spoke up.

"Wait a minute! I forgot my fish stringer! Here, Josh, hold my spear gun while I run back to my condo and get it."

Josh and Tank stood looking at each other silently until Macho started running barefoot down the outside, concrete steps. Then Tank asked softly, "Why'd you say a dumb thing like that? You know it's too dangerous for us to go down in that sub! We're too inexperienced! Snorkeling at the surface and shallow scuba dives are one thing, but going for the *Bluegill* is crazy!"

Josh was stung and a little irritated at Tank's words. "Crazy?" he said. "You mean you're afraid to make the dive!"

"No, I'm not afraid, but I'm not stupid, either!"

Josh's rare temper began to slip. "You saying I'm stupid?"

Tank's voice speeded up as *his* anger showed. "No, I said I wasn't stupid! And I don't think you are, either. But you're acting sorta different around this new kid."

Josh snapped, "Well, I'm not different. I'm just not as chicken as some people!"

Tank took a slow, deep breath, his face clouding.

"Maybe you'd better go with Macho by yourself, Josh!" he said. Then he turned and reentered the Catlett condo, slamming the door shut behind him.

Twenty minutes later, Josh and Macho were swimming well out into the bay with their snorkel gear and fins. Josh felt strange not having Tank at his side. They had been best friends almost since they were babies, and while they'd had arguments now and then—even a couple of scuffles—they'd never really had a serious argument.

Oh, well, Josh told himself, *even if he's mad, he'll soon get over it. And he won't tell about the tape. But I've got to stay close to Macho to make sure he doesn't tell anybody.*

Through his swim mask, Josh watched Macho moving cautiously through the clear Pacific waters. Macho's black fins swiftly propelled him toward a large fish. From his study of Hawaii's fish, Josh recognized the quarry as a peacock grouper.

Josh had never speared a fish, and he flinched when Macho's weapon fired. The dark-colored fish with its hundreds of blue, starlike spots jerked violently when the spear struck.

Josh treaded water as Macho's fins propelled him to Josh's side. As the boys brought their heads out of the water and took out their snorkel mouthpieces, Macho took the fish off the spear, put it on his three-foot-long stringer, and handed it to Josh. "Tie the stringer to your waist," he instructed.

Josh started to shake his head, remembering how the local kids handle speared fish. It's dangerous to keep any such fish close to them, so the locals float an old inner tube on the surface. Any fish taken are quickly removed from the water and dropped into a bucket suspended in the tube. That keeps any smell of blood from getting into the ocean and possibly attracting sharks.

Before Josh could say anything, however, Macho turned, reinserted his mouthpiece, and swam away, reloading his sling gun.

Josh put his own mouthpiece back in and stuck his face below the surface to follow Macho's movements. Then he looped one end of the stringer around his waist just above his blue swim trunks. As he tied the knot he thought, *I sure hope that fish's struggle didn't attract any—uh-oh!*

His eyes opened wide as a long, slender shape appeared from the distant blue and headed straight for him. Josh instantly recognized the distinctive stripes along its side. Terrified words exploded in his mind.

Tiger shark!

Chapter Three

ARRIVAL OF A STRANGER

Through his face mask, Josh's wide eyes watched the great predator's swift approach. The shark was about ten feet long. It swam purposefully, effortlessly. Large, black eyes focused on the boy treading water.

Josh forgot all about the speared fish tied to the stringer around his waist. He saw only the long, slender beast with its striped side that clearly identified it as a tiger shark. Josh remembered to not act panicky. He kept his fins moving slowly, methodically, as though he weren't scared to death.

Josh knew that shark attacks in Hawaii are rare. But this predator streaked toward Josh so fast that he was sure he was going to be seriously injured. The boy was afraid to take his eyes off the shark to look for Macho. He wanted to watch the tiger's every move until he could think of a way to defend himself without a weapon.

However, out of the corner of his left eye, Josh saw the older boy. His back was turned, so he couldn't see Josh's danger.

About twenty feet from the boy, the shark suddenly veered off to the right. Josh turned with the beast, watching as it swam slowly in a complete circle.

Maybe he's just checking me out, Josh told himself hopefully, his heart racing. He was still so concerned over the shark's presence that the speared peacock grouper on his waist stringer was forgotten. *Maybe he'll go away—oh, no!* The tiger shark again streaked straight toward Josh!

The defenseless boy could only think to bring up his black-finned feet and kick at the shark. It swerved quickly to the right, flashed thirty feet away, and slowed. Very methodically, it again circled the boy. He turned in the water, always facing the predator.

With every passing second, Josh grew more afraid watching his silent stalker. Then he felt a glimmer of hope. *It's swimming away!* he told himself joyfully. *If it keeps going—it's turning back!*

The shark whipped around sharply and shot toward the boy. Josh watched in terror as the animal passed about twenty feet below him. He prayed silently, *Oh, Lord! Don't let him get me!*

Josh continued to tread water carefully, avoiding the erratic movements that might trigger an instant attack. He was quickly reviewing everything he'd learned about how to respond to the presence of sharks when he realized, *Here he comes again!*

The shark was amazingly fast for such a big animal.

It rushed up at a forty-five degree angle straight toward the helpless boy. This time the shark did not stop or veer away!

Josh tried desperately to bring up his fins to kick at his tormentor, but he was too slow. The shark hurtled upward so fast that the boy barely had time to lash out franically with his bare hands.

The shark's mouth opened wide as he struck. Josh caught a glimpse of terrible teeth as the great jaws snapped shut. Josh felt the shark's rough skin against his rib cage. The predator didn't stop and tear, as Josh had expected, but flashed on past and behind the boy. Josh didn't feel any pain, but he looked in fear of what he would see of his side.

Suddenly, Josh was jerked violently backward and down and towed through the sea. He swiveled his head and saw that the shark was swimming away powerfully, the speared fish in its mouth.

It didn't bite me! It took the fish! Josh's relieved mind screamed. *But the grouper's on the stringer, and that's tied to my waist! I'm being towed so fast the shark'll drown me! I've got to get away and have some air!*

Josh grabbed for the stringer at his waist, but he couldn't break it. In snorkeling, he didn't carry a knife as he did when scuba diving.

Josh struggled with the stringer. *Can't break it! I'm losing strength fast! If I don't breathe—*

Suddenly the terrifying backward towing stopped. It

had lasted only a few seconds but seemed like minutes. Josh glimpsed the end of the stringer floating back from the shark's jaws. *He must have bitten the stringer through! Air! I've got to breathe!*

Josh kicked for the surface, strong legs driving the fins fast. He felt the snorkel clear the surface. With a quick, explosive puff, he blew out water in the snorkel and expelled the remaining air in his lungs. As he broke the surface, he jerked his mouthpiece out and hungrily sucked in great, welcome gulps of fresh air.

Thanks, Lord! he prayed silently.

Macho surfaced fifty yards away and removed his mask. "Hey, Josh!" he called out. "What are you doing over there?"

For a second, Josh almost made an angry, sarcastic reply. Then relief flooded over him at being alive. He began to laugh.

"What's so funny?" Macho asked after swimming over to Josh with the spear gun in his hand.

"Let's go ashore and I'll tell you."

A few minutes later, the boys pulled their cutoffs over their wet swim trunks. Josh slipped his loose-fitting aloha shirt* on, but Macho remained bare-chested. The boys stretched out on the sandy beach near a coconut tree. By then, Josh was summarizing his experience with the tiger shark.

"That last time, when he came at me so fast and I saw those jaws open and felt his rough skin against my side,

I thought I was a goner!" Josh added ruefully, "I'm never going to keep a speared fish near me again!"

"Well, after that," Macho said with a grin, "diving to that sub in Lahaina* Harbor should seem a lot less scary."

Josh didn't even want to think about diving 135 feet to the *Bluegill*. He didn't want to think about the mystery submarine he had seen sink. He didn't want to think about the secret he was keeping from his family.

Aloud he said, "I'd go down if I could, but we'll probably never get the chance."

"We'll make the chance! In fact, we'd better do it pretty soon—before the Navy raises the *Bluegill* so nobody can ever dive to her again."

"What'll they do with her?"

"My father says they'll cut her up, take the pieces farther out to sea, and sink them forever."

Josh wished they'd do that before he was forced to dive to the sub, but he didn't say that. Instead, he stood and brushed the sand from his legs. "I've got to be getting back. Uh, could we go by your condo so I can get my videotape back?"

"Why? Don't you trust me with it?"

"It's not that. I'd just feel better if I had it hidden someplace where only I knew where it was."

Macho also stood. His eyes narrowed suspiciously. "You really *don't* trust me yet, do you? Well, you can have your tape back!"

"No need to get upset," Josh said as they turned toward

the condos.

"It's okay, Josh! In five minutes, you'll have your tape back. Then you'll feel better!"

Josh did feel better when he held the videocassette again. He slipped it inside the waistband of his cutoffs. When he dropped his aloha shirt over it, there was no sign of the cassette.

Josh felt guilty doing that, especially when he entered the condo and all his family were home. He heard the television newscaster from Honolulu and stopped to listen.

"Government sources today refused to confirm rumors that the CIA is actively working with the Navy to locate and recover a submarine that reportedly sank somewhere off the coast of Maui* yesterday. Authorities also refused to comment on speculation that the sunken vessel belongs to the Soviet Union."

Nathan looked up from where he was sprawled on his stomach, watching the TV. "Hi, Josh," he said.

"Shh!" Josh replied. "I want to hear this."

The newscaster continued, "However, records show that the CIA was an active participant in a similar incident some years ago when a Soviet submarine exploded and sank in Hawaiian waters.

"Veteran members of the news media here in the state capital are suggesting there's a quiet but desperate race on between the superpowers to find the sub first. It's believed that it would carry the latest Soviet submarine technology, which could be invaluable to American intelligence sources."

As the newscaster changed subjects, Nathan lifted the remote control device and snapped the set off. He turned to his older brother and said, "Hey, Josh, Dad says this place will be crawling with spies looking for that sub!"

Mr. Ladd came out of the back bedroom. "Now, Nathan," he said, "don't go putting words in my mouth."

"Well, that's what you meant," Nathan replied. "Boy! Wouldn't it be something to see a real, live spy?"

Mr. Ladd moved to the head of the table nearest the lanai.* "Mary," he asked, "you ready for all of us to sit down?"

Mrs. Ladd handed a platter of fresh vegetables across the counter in the pass-through between kitchen and dining room. "Yes, Dear," she answered. "Tiffany, please set these on the table."

"Yuck! Vegetables!" Nathan said, making a face.

"At the prices we pay here in Hawaii, they're more like gold nuggets than tomatoes and cucumbers," his mother replied. "Josh, where are you going?"

"Uh, to wash up."

"Well, please hurry and sit down at the table."

In the bathroom he shared with Nathan, Josh decided the safest place for the video was in the cupboard below the sink, against the back wall behind the pipes. *I'll have to find a better place so Nathan won't find it, but this'll do for now,* Josh assured himself. His little brother sometimes prowled through Josh's belongings in spite of warnings from their parents.

The meal was nearly over when Josh thought of a plan to keep from having to dive on the *Bluegill* with Macho. It was a simple idea, but Josh was sure it would work. He thought, *I'll talk about Macho's plan to dive to the sub, then ask for permission to join him. Naturally, Dad and Mom won't let me, so I'll have a good excuse to give Macho.*

A moment later, Mr. Ladd exclaimed in disbelief, "Macho's going to do what? Don't his parents know what that boy does?"

Before Josh could reply, his mother added, "That dive's much too dangerous for Macho! And when're we going to get to meet him and his parents?"

"I don't know," Josh said. Then he added, "I suppose that means you wouldn't let me join him if he does dive on the *Bluegill.*"

"Of course not, Josh," his father said. "Don't you understand the dangers? I stopped by the library a while today and read microfilm of old Honolulu newspapers about why our navy sank the *Bluegill.* The original plan was to use it to practice rescuing people from a sunken sub. But that was before scuba gear made it possible for almost anybody to dive that deep.

"There was also an article in this morning's newspaper. Health officers said that several cases of the bends have resulted from diving to that sub. Personally, I'll be glad when the *Bluegill* is raised."

"What's 'bends'?" Nathan asked.

"That's when a diver comes up too fast from deep down," Tiffany answered. "Bubbles get in the blood and cause terrible pain."

"A diver can die from the bends," Mr. Ladd said, folding his napkin and placing it beside his plate. "But there are other dangers in diving to that old sub, too.

"I once interviewed a diver for an article in our paper. He said he'd been inside the *Bluegill*. It'd been stripped, of course, before it was sunk. But lots of old pieces of pipe and steel things were sticking out where a person's diving gear could get caught. And there's also a dangerous chemical reaction between the sea water and the acid from the sub's batteries, which weren't removed."

"I thought World War II submarines were diesel-powered," Josh said.

"They were, but they carried batteries for auxiliary power. Well, I hate to eat and run, but I've got to get moving."

"I thought this was supposed to be a vacation, John," his wife said.

"It is, but I've got some work to do, too. I'm trying to set up an interview with the commander of the local Coast Guard station on boat safety. Might as well take advantage of being here to get a good story."

Mr. Ladd glanced around the condo and added, "Too bad this place doesn't have a phone. Guess I'll have to go down to the ground floor and use the pay phone by the elevator. Well, see all of you later."

Josh finished eating and went downstairs to the beach. He watched two local fishermen with an old-fashioned washtub and an off-white net. They waded slowly in the shallow waters of Maalaea Bay* not fifty feet from shore.

"Hey, Josh!" someone called. Josh turned to see Macho stretched out on a pale blue, plastic-webbed chaise longue in the shade of a palm tree. "Pull up a seat by me," Macho said.

Josh dragged another webbed chair over and sat down just as an attractive woman in her twenties walked across the grass. She wore an orange, "neon," one-piece bathing suit.

"Hi," she said with a warm smile after stopping beside the boys. "Is the water cold?"

"No, it's perfect," Josh assured her.

"This is my first trip to the islands," she said, looking uncertainly at the bay. "Is it safe to swim here?"

"Sure!" Macho answered. "Perfectly safe."

"Thank you," the woman said, smiling again. She turned back toward the beach, then stopped and said, "I'm Nancy Hogan. Staying in the end condo."

"I'm Josh. He's called Macho."

The three talked briefly, then the woman waded into the water. At the same moment, Josh saw Tank. He was talking to Igor Petrov.

"Look who your friend's talking to!" Macho

whispered. "Wonder why they're watching us?"

Josh thought of the coordinates he had memorized where a submarine sank. Then he tried to shake off the thought that suddenly jumped into his head. *Nah! Tank gave his word! He wouldn't tell, even if he is mad at me.*

"Igor sure doesn't look like a spy," Macho said softly, interrupting Josh's thoughts. "But that's the trouble with spies—nobody can tell who might be one."

Josh glanced around to make sure nobody was close enough to overhear. Even so, he also whispered as he replied, "Well, Tank won't tell anybody about my tape or what I know."

"That's good! The only way a Soviet agent could know would be if either I or Tank talked. I haven't told anyone!"

Josh tried not to think of Tank's talking to Igor. But as he watched Nancy Hogan swimming strongly in the bay, the idea crossed his mind, *Maybe I should make up with Tank.*

Macho again interrupted Josh's thoughts to say, "If Tank *did* tell, and Igor *is* a spy, you wouldn't know it until it's too late."

"It's okay, I tell you! Tank's my friend! He'll keep a secret."

"I sure hope so, Josh. You're already in enough trouble without having a friend turn on you."

Josh nodded and tried to concentrate on the fishermen with their net and Nancy Hogan's swimming. Yet a strange uneasiness kept him from really enjoying the sight. "I'll ask Tank," he finally told Macho.

"Good idea! If he's told Igor anything, you can think of something to protect yourself in case Igor is a spy."

Josh nodded, feeling uncomfortable at the thought of what Tank would say when Josh asked him if he'd betrayed a secret. *But I've got to know for sure!* Josh decided.

"He'll be mad," Macho warned, reading Josh's frown.

"Probably."

When Igor walked back toward the condo, Josh got up and slowly approached Tank. He didn't smile at Josh. That gave Josh a sick, sad feeling.

Chapter Four

OLD NEWSPAPERS & NEW DANGERS

Josh stopped in front of Tank, who was spreading a large beach towel over a folding lounge chair. "Hi," Josh said, feeling the uneasiness between them.

"Hi," Tank replied as he settled onto the chair. "How'd your dive with Macho go?"

Usually, Josh would have been bursting to tell Tank about the encounter with the tiger shark. But not this time. Describing that incident would only make Tank think Josh had let Macho talk him into doing something foolish. So Josh shrugged and said, "Okay, I guess. I saw you talking to Igor."

Tank's eyes narrowed slightly, and he nodded.

Josh shifted uneasily from one bare foot to the other, his eyes on the ground, as he continued, "I just wondered what you were talking about."

"Nothing much."

The coolness between the two longtime friends bothered Josh a lot. Still, he had to know what he had come to ask. "You say anything about—you know what?"

Tank jerked himself upright in the chair. "You mean about the sub?"

"Shh!" Josh leaned forward and whispered, "Not so loud!"

For a moment, Tank's eyes half closed in thought. Then he said, "You think maybe I told him, don't you?"

Josh squirmed, uncomfortable with the pain in Tank's voice. "Well, no—I mean, I just wanted to know for sure," he said defensively. "That's all."

Slowly, Tank got to his feet and looked straight into Josh's eyes. "Macho made you think that, didn't he?"

Josh started to deny it, then hesitated, unsure of whose idea it really was.

"I never thought I'd see the day you'd take the word of a stranger over mine!" Tank went on. "If you think I even *might* give away a secret, you're not the friend I thought you were!" With that, he grabbed his beach towel and hurried away.

Josh called after him, "Hey, wait, Tank!" But Tank didn't stop. Josh felt a sick loneliness inside.

That evening, Josh was strangely silent. His parents questioned him about it, but he insisted nothing was wrong. When the late TV news came on, the top story again concerned the submarine search. "Informed sources who asked not to be identified today indicated that the submarine is suspected of being a new, secret, unmanned Soviet robot...."

"Unmanned?" Josh's father said, turning down the

volume when the station went to a commercial break. "Do all of you realize what that means if it's true? Do you understand why our country *must* find that sunken sub before the Russians do?"

Nathan moved his head behind Josh's shoulders and whispered, "No, but I think we're going to find out."

He was right. John Ladd talked about the reason nations gather information about all other nations, both allies and potential enemies. Ordinarily, Josh wouldn't have cared too much, but his secret knowledge of the missing sub's location made him keenly aware of his personal involvement.

"If that sub can function without a human crew," his father concluded, "whatever country it belongs to— including the Soviet Union—can take chances that aren't possible with people on board. A sub like that could try an attack that would be suicidal for a human crew."

Josh glanced out the sliding lanai* door at Maalaea Bay.* Both Kahoolawe* and Molokini* could be seen in the distance. Just beyond them, the ocean held a secret that only he knew.

His father continued with some feeling. "Why, if there are enough robot subs, they could do incredible damage to our country—or any other—in a surprise attack. It's absolutely critical that our people find that sub first so they can learn how it works and plan a defense against it!"

Josh's guilty conscience made him jump up so quickly he almost knocked over the floor lamp.

"Careful, Son!" his father warned. "This place is rented. We don't want to have to pay breakage on things!"

"Yeah!" Nathan added. "Where're you going in such a hurry?"

"Uh, to get a drink of water."

It hurt to lie, but he hurried inside the bathroom and closed the door. Leaning back against it, he felt all mixed up and sick inside. After waiting half a minute to calm down, he bent over, opened the door under the sink, and checked the videocassette.

At least Nathan didn't find it, Josh told himself. *But the way he prowls through my things, I'd better hide this someplace better until I can straighten out this mess.*

As Josh came out of the bathroom with the cassette under his shirt, his father called, "Son, I arranged that interview with the commander of the Coast Guard station. You want to go with me?"

"I guess so," Josh answered without enthusiasm.

"Good! Now, if you don't mind, I'd like you and Tank to do some more research at the library in Wailuku.* You boys would enjoy knowing more about that first sub that sank years ago. Then you'll better understand why finding this latest one is so important. I can write a story for our paper, too."

"Aw, Dad, I don't want to. Besides, Tank's been acting funny lately."

Josh was always amazed at how his parents seemed to sense things. His father now asked quietly, "You two have a falling out?"

Keeping his back turned to the living room so his family couldn't see the bulge under his shirt, Josh said, "Sorta, I guess."

"Over Macho, I'll bet!" Nathan exclaimed.

Josh didn't answer but started into his bedroom. His father's voice followed. "When are your mother and I going to get to meet this new friend? How about inviting him and his parents over so we can all get acquainted?"

"I'll ask him tomorrow, Dad," Josh said. Then he closed the door and pulled the draperies shut so the strong trade winds wouldn't blow them back and let a passerby see what he was doing. Looking around carefully, Josh thought, *Now where can I hide this tape so Nathan won't find it?*

It took a while to make up his mind, but Josh finally decided. He pulled the small chest of drawers away from the wall. *That'll work,* he said to himself, *but how can I keep it there? Oh, I know!* He shoved the chest back into place and returned to his father to ask, "Dad, do you have some cellophane tape in your attache case?"

"Of course, Son. Help yourself." Josh's father always carried tape in his briefcase to hold pieces of ad layouts in place when he made presentations to potential advertisers. And wherever he went, even on vacation, he carried his briefcase.

Josh took the tape back into the bedroom, closed the door, and pulled the chest out again. Then he carefully secured the light video box to the back of it. *There!* he thought with satisfaction, shoving the chest against the wall. *Nobody'll find that, not even my nosy little brother.*

Early the next morning, while the clouds were still ringing the massive shoulders of Haleakala* east of the bay, Josh punched the elevator button for the ride to the parking lot. The door slid open, and Josh started to step in, but he stopped at the sight of Igor Petrov.

Josh quickly tried to think of something to say to keep from riding down with the man, but he drew a blank. So he got in, and the door closed behind him.

Igor leaned down and whispered in his raspy voice, "Ve got to talk."

Josh's heart jumped. Did Igor know the secret? "Uh, I'm in a hurry," Josh stammered.

"Ve talk! Ven? Vere?" An urgency in Igor's voice concerned Josh.

"Uh, soon—maybe."

The elevator stopped, and the door drew open. Josh hurried out, hearing the man call, "Please! Must talk!"

Scurrying across the parking lot, Josh pretended not to hear, his mind in a turmoil. *What's he want to talk about? If he knows, either Tank or Macho told! Oh, why me? I'm getting in deeper and deeper!*

"Hey, Josh!" a familiar voice shouted. "Where you going in such a hurry?"

Josh turned around to see Macho cutting across the parking lot toward him. "Oh, hi," Josh replied. "Guess

I was lost in thought. But say, how about bringing your parents over so mine can meet you and them?"

Macho shook his head and answered, "My dad works crazy hours, so I don't know when he'll be home. Mom's big in her club work, so she's not home a whole lot, either."

"You mean your parents don't know where you are most of the time?"

"I told you before, I'm my own man. I can take care of myself."

Josh started to say his parents always knew where he was, and with whom, but he caught himself. That wasn't quite true since he had started spending time with Macho.

"I'm going to the library to learn more about that first Soviet sub that sank off Hawaii years ago," Macho said, changing the subject. "Nancy Hogan offered to drive me. Want to come along?"

"That's funny," Josh replied. "That's what my father suggested I do."

"Great! Here comes Nancy now. Let's go."

"Soon's I tell my mom." Josh started to run back to the elevator and then stopped at the sight of his sister moving along the fourth-story walkway. He cupped his hands and called, "Hey, Tif! Tell Mom I'm going to the library with Macho. Nancy Hogan's going to take us."

Josh felt he didn't need to ask permission since his father had suggested the research and Josh had told his parents about meeting Nancy. But when Josh looked at

Macho, he saw disapproval in the older boy's eyes. Then he remembered Macho's words: "I'm my own man." Josh realized he had just gone down a notch in Macho's eyes, and he didn't like the feeling.

But how come Igor's trying to talk to me? Josh asked himself, forcing his mind onto another subject as Nancy stopped and the boys got into her car. *Tank says he didn't tell him my secret, so I'd better double-check on Macho, but I can't do that with Nancy around.*

On the first part of the drive along a narrow, two-lane, paved road slicing through sugarcane and pineapple fields, Nancy asked, "What takes you boys to the library so early?"

"We're going to do research into that Soviet sub that sank off the islands a few years back," Macho explained.

Josh jabbed his elbow into Macho's ribs as discreetly as possible so Nancy wouldn't see. "My father owns a tourist publication," Josh added. "He suggested we do some library research."

It was all true, yet Josh knew it wasn't quite the whole truth. Still, he didn't want anyone to guess why he was really so interested in a sunken submarine.

Nancy asked a few more casual questions, but when neither boy seemed interested in talking further, she changed the subject. The three talked about the weather, the cane fields still being harvested and other superficial things all the way to the library, where she dropped them off. As the boys entered, Josh stopped and looked back.

Igor was just parking his old car under a monkeypod*
tree in the library parking lot. *Wonder if he's followed
us?* Josh asked himself. *Does he know or not?*

As the boys headed for the microfilm area, Josh asked
Macho casually, "You talk to Igor much?"

"That old guy?" Macho answered with scorn. "We've
got nothing to talk about. Anyway, he barely speaks
English."

Satisfied, Josh asked the librarian for the newspaper in-
dex. Mr. Ladd had taught Josh how to find old newspaper
stories under a given heading, like "submarines." Macho
also knew, so when the boys found logical headings, they
asked the librarian for the appropriate microfilm reels.
She helped thread the reels onto two viewing machines
and showed the boys where to insert coins to make
photocopies of any pages they wanted. Then she left them
seated before the two units.

A little while later, Macho exclaimed, "Here's
something! Look!"

Josh got up from his machine and looked at Macho's
screen. The article displayed there told of the sinking of
a Soviet submarine near Hawaii back in 1968.

Josh finished reading the story and returned to his
machine. A few minutes later he called Macho over.
"Here's more!" he said. He pointed to a March 19, 1975,
story in the *Honolulu Advertiser* that read, "The Central
Intelligence Agency (CIA) recovered part of a sunken
Soviet submarine which yielded military secrets with pro-

found national security implications, the *Los Angeles Times* has confirmed."

Quickly, both boys skimmed the story. The sunken sub was a 320-foot-long, diesel-powered craft. It exploded and sank near Hawaii seven years before the article was written.

Josh's eyes darted around the old newspaper story on the screen: "nuclear-tipped missiles.... CIA agents on the verge of breaking the Russian intelligence code, which had been a mystery to U.S. cryptographers...," and so on.

A story in the same paper two days later said that if the reports were true, the U.S. had recovered just about all the submarine and possibly the code machine. That meant intelligence officers could unscramble all the secret messages the sub would have received. However, both the White House and the CIA refused comment.

Josh became so caught up in what all this meant to him personally that he hurriedly scanned all other related stories. Every report made him more anxious about what a powerful secret he had—and the dangers it presented.

The recovery efforts in the 1968 sub sinking had been carefully cloaked in secrecy and had never come to light. "The CIA sure kept the lid down tight on that story," Josh told Macho.

"Well, that's not true about the *Bluegill*," Macho replied. "These microfilms tell how it served in World War II, was decommissioned and deliberately sunk off Lahaina,* and how the Navy's now planning to raise it."

The boys made their last photocopy of old newspaper stories and returned the microfilm. As they moved away from the librarian's desk, Josh whispered, "This is too big and dangerous for us kids! It's even international. I've *got* to tell my folks!"

Macho whispered back, "You can't tell! Have you forgotten what will happen to you *and* them if the Soviets find out what you know?"

Josh started to reply, then stopped and stared. "Hey, there's Igor at the far end of the library!" he said. "I think he's been watching us!"

"Let's see if he follows us!" Macho suggested.

The boys walked out with their photocopies. As the outside glass door swung open, Josh saw Igor reflected there. "He's following us, Macho!"

Just as they reached the street corner, a car pulled up to the curb. "I thought that was you," Nancy Hogan said from behind the wheel. "Want a ride home? I'm on my way back to the condo."

"Sure do!" both boys replied together. They slid into the front seat and buckled up. As the car pulled away, Josh and Macho looked back at Igor.

"Something the matter?" Nancy asked.

"Oh, no!" Josh said quickly. "Everything's fine now!" He slid his photocopied pages behind his back, between himself and the front seat, and repeated, "Just fine!"

He was wrong—very wrong.

Chapter Five

WINDSURFING TO DISASTER

Josh watched the six o'clock network news that night. "Unnamed sources today reported Soviet surface craft have been spotted heading toward Maui,*" the anchorwoman said.

"Maui?" Nathan repeated in surprise. "That's where we are!"

"Shh!" Josh replied. "Listen!"

The announcer continued, "It is believed these ships will be used in helping search for a missing submarine that now is generally thought to be a Soviet robot vessel. Records show that this same pattern was followed in 1968, when a Russian submarine sank off Oahu.*

"The Soviets launched an extensive search at that time, but they apparently never pinpointed the sub's location several miles down in the ocean. However, the U.S. Navy did locate and recover at least part of the sub, although the CIA went to great lengths to prevent full knowledge of the mission from becoming public."

"I read about that today in the old newspaper files at

the library," Josh said.

His father turned down the TV and replied, "Good work, Son. I'd like to see the photocopies you made."

Josh handed them to his father, who skimmed over them and then passed them to his wife and Nathan. Tiffany was swimming in the bay with Tank's sister.

When the sheets were returned to Josh, he thumbed through them, frowning. "Hmm," he said, "I seem to be missing one page that I remember photocopying. It said something about how in 1971 the Navy's Pacific command reported the largest force of Soviet ships ever sighted in Hawaii."

"I remember that," his father said. "Apparently they were looking for their sunken sub at the same time our navy was recovering it. But the sub must have sunk well out to sea, as I suspect the robot one did this week."

Josh stirred uneasily, knowing that wasn't true. He wanted so much to tell his parents the whole story, because everything was getting worse.

A couple of years before, Josh's father had said of another problem the boy had, "You're not a bad person, Son, but you did make a mistake in judgment. You chose expediency over our Christian principles." Josh had a feeling he was making another such mistake, but how could he get out of it?

John Ladd changed the subject. "Oh, Josh, I got that appointment with the Coast Guard officer. Be ready in the morning and you can go along on the interview."

The commander was a tall, handsome man in neat uniform who welcomed father and son to his small office early the next day. After getting acquainted, Mr. Ladd produced a tape recorder. "Mind if I tape this interview?" he asked. "It will help me to quote you accurately."

"Not at all."

Josh's father turned on the machine and began asking questions about boating safety. The officer answered them easily and handed some printed material on the subject to Mr. Ladd.

When his father seemed satisfied and about to turn off the recorder, Josh spoke up. "Could you tell us some true stories about rescues you've made, Sir?"

Mr. Ladd nodded approval, and the officer recalled stories of fighting shipboard fires, going on search-and-rescue missions, and saving people from vessels sinking in heavy surf.

"Wow!" Josh exclaimed during a lull. "That's exciting!"

The commander smiled across his desk. "It's not all that way, of course. For example, sometimes boaters accidentally turn on their emergency indicator beacons."

"What's that?" the boy asked.

"It's a tube-shaped device about a foot long and four inches across and weighs a pound or so. It has a wire for a transmitting antenna so the unit can send an emergency radio signal if someone's in distress. It's usually orange, although I've seen a few red ones. It's activated by flipping a switch or by being turned upside down, as when a boat capsizes.

"The signal is received in Honolulu, where they use a kind of direction finder to locate the signal's source. We've been able to rescue distressed boaters that way because we always investigate. That's true even though some funny things happen."

"Like what?" Josh prompted.

"Well, once we followed the signal along the road up into the Maui highlands. We knocked on the door of a private residence and said, 'Sir, are you aware your emergency distress signal is activated in the boat parked in your garage?' "

Josh and his father laughed, thanked the officer, and left, feeling good about the stories Mr. Ladd could write for his paper.

As father and son entered the condo on their return, Nathan stood on the small lanai* with binoculars focused across the bay. "Hey, look at that!" he cried, pointing where he had been looking. "Ships! All kinds of big ships. See? Just beyond Molokini* and Kahoolawe!* Are they Russian, Dad?"

His father took the glasses and focused on the distant ships. "They're ours! I wonder what they're doing so close to shore?"

"Do you suppose that submarine sank right out there?" Mary Ladd asked, coming up behind them.

"I hope it did!" Nathan exclaimed. "We'd have a front-row seat! And wouldn't it be neat if the Russians showed up at the same time?"

"Let's pray that doesn't happen," his father said softly. "It could cause an international incident—or worse."

Josh felt his insides twist. He took the binoculars and focused on the ships. He knew why they were there.

Just then a firm knock sounded at the front door. Mr. Ladd went to open it.

"John Ladd?" a man's voice asked.

There was something about the authoritative tone that startled Josh. He lowered the binoculars and turned around. A tall, slender man in a summer-weight suit stood there.

"Would you mind stepping outside for a moment, please, Mr. Ladd?" the man said. Josh felt a frightened shiver sweep over his body as his father complied and closed the door after himself.

"I wonder who that is?" Mrs. Ladd said.

Josh had a terrible feeling he knew. He thought, *That's a government official. He must be asking Dad if he saw or heard anything when we were on that fishing boat. I'll bet they're asking everyone who was out there. They probably got their names from each skipper. That means— they'll ask me, too!*

Josh was sure of it when he saw his father and the stranger walking to the middle of the parking lot.

"They're standing out there where nobody can hear them, huh?" Nathan observed.

"Probably," Josh replied with a dry mouth.

The three Ladd family members watched until the well-dressed stranger walked away and Mr. Ladd headed back for the condo. His wife and sons met him at the door.

"What was that all about, Dad?" Nathan asked excitedly.

"I'm sorry, but I can't tell anyone."

"I know! Spies!" Nathan yelled. "That man was a spy, and he wanted to know if you'd seen any other spies around here, huh, Dad?"

His father rumpled the boy's hair and smiled faintly as he replied, "No need guessing. I can't tell you."

Josh had been sure he knew what the man wanted, but why hadn't he questioned Josh, too?

I think, he told himself, *all the fishermen signed some kind of insurance release when they went aboard. The skipper would have their names and addresses on that. But I was only going for the ride, so I didn't sign anything. If the skipper and Dad also forgot to mention it, that would explain things.*

Josh shook his head, wondering if the stranger would eventually find out and come looking for him. *What'll I tell him?* Josh asked himself. *I don't want to lie, but I'm afraid to tell the whole story, too!*

Tiffany came in just then, her hair wet from swimming. "Josh, I saw Macho downstairs," she told him. "He said to ask you if you'd like to practice buddy breathing with him in the bay."

Josh decided he'd talk to Macho and Tank again about the need to tell his folks about the video and what he knew. After that, he would tell his parents. He hurried outside and took the elevator at the far end of the condo. It stopped at the second floor, and Igor Petrov got on. Josh felt sweat break out on his forehead at the idea of being trapped alone with him.

As the door started to slide shut, the man said in his heavy accent, "T'ings not alvays vat seem."

Without answering, Josh threw his right hand out and hit the side of the door. It stopped instantly and then re-opened. As it did, Josh leaped out. He heard Igor call, "Vait!" But Josh ran to the outside concrete stairs and hurried down to meet Macho.

The two boys helped each other get ready for their prac-tice scuba dive. They checked their own equipment and then each other's, making sure everything was operating properly. Then they swam out into the bay to where the water was just over their heads.

Josh asked, "You ready?" When Macho nodded, Josh added, "Just remember what we learned in training. First you pretend you're low on air, and I'll share my air with you. Then we reverse. Okay?"

They dived to the bottom to rehearse a procedure that might save a diver's life. The idea was simple: Macho indicated by hand signals that he was low on air. Josh removed the regulator from his mouth and allowed Macho to breathe from his tank. Then the roles were switched.

When the boys surfaced and removed their regulators, Josh said, "I just hope we never need to do that for real!"

"It's easy," Macho said with a shrug.

"It was easy because this is shallow water and close to shore, with both of us having plenty of air. But if we were way out somewhere and down deep, we'd both be low on air. It might not be so easy to share when one guy's out of air and the other one's almost out."

"I wouldn't have any trouble," Macho said confidently, starting to swim toward shore.

Josh saw his opportunity. As soon as they were ashore and started to remove their scuba gear, he said as casually as he could manage, "Speaking of trouble, I really think I should tell my parents about what I saw."

The older boy shook his head. "You can't do that! You swore to keep it secret."

Josh wanted to explain how guilty he felt about not being honest with his family. But he also felt he couldn't fully trust Macho, which meant he didn't want to risk making him unhappy. So he asked, "Why should you care? I'm the only one in danger."

"That's where you're wrong!" Macho said. "You're forgetting your family will also be in danger if you don't keep that secret! If Soviet agents knew about the tape and that you know exactly where their sub sank, do you think they'd just come after you? No way! They'd go for your whole family, figuring you've told them everything or else threatening to hurt them as a way to make you talk. You

don't want to put them in that kind of danger, do you?"
Josh frowned, considering once again how real that threat
might be.

"Of course," Macho added with a sly smile, "I could
tell someone the secret if you made me mad or
something."

"You wouldn't!"

"Just kidding! Just kidding!" Macho said. But then he
added quickly, "Now, when're we going to make that dive
to the *Bluegill*?"

Josh looked in disbelief at the other boy before answering, "That sounds like blackmail, Macho!"

"I think of it as giving somebody a choice," Macho
said, smirking.

"But that's a dangerous dive!" Josh protested. "We're
both inexperienced! I think we should try something else
first. Besides, I asked my parents about it, and they said
no."

"You're not afraid, are you?"

"It's not that, Macho! It's just smart to know as much
as possible about the dive before we make it. I also don't
like to disobey my parents."

"Well, I'm my own man," Macho said proudly. "I don't
need my parents' permission to make the dive. Any guy
who's a close friend of mine makes *his* own decisions,
too."

Josh groaned inwardly as he realized his parents' refusal
to let him dive on the *Bluegill* wouldn't sway Macho. His

mind grabbed quickly for another excuse to use. "Shouldn't we at least ask someone who's done it what it's like?" he said.

"Wouldn't hurt, I guess. I know this dive-shop operator in Lahaina* who said he led a bunch of guys in a dive to the *Bluegill*. Okay, we'll ask him. Then we go down ourselves."

Josh hoped the dive-shop operator would advise firmly against the dive. Josh thought about praying this would happen, but he hadn't felt much like praying lately. He hadn't even read his Bible the last few mornings, feeling uncomfortable with what he was doing. Now Macho was threatening him, too. He shuddered involuntarily as he thought, *This is just one more problem I don't know how to handle!*

Later that day, the boys rode into Lahaina with Mrs. Ladd, who was going shopping. She dropped them off on Front Street.

Both sides of the street were lined with shops catering to tourists. The ocean was only a few feet away. Countless small boats were anchored between Lahaina and the island of Lanai. Multicolored parasails* showed above powerboats towing thrill-seekers into the sky. The boys crossed the street toward the mountains that rose directly behind the old whaling town.

Inside the dive shop, Macho introduced Josh to Thad Ruskin. Josh liked the forty-year-old dive-shop operator who said he had logged five thousand dives. His long, narrow store was filled with everything for divers, including color-coordinated wetsuits for the increasing number of women divers.

When Thad had examined and returned the boys' certification cards, he asked, "What can I do for you?"

Josh wandered a few feet away, looking at the face masks, buoyancy control devices, air-tank backpacks, hoses, regulators and other diving gear. Macho urged, "Tell us about some of the dives you've made to the *Bluegill*."

"I get so many tourists in here without sufficient experience who want to make the dive to that old sub!" Thad said with a shake of his head. "I won't take them. It's too dangerous."

Josh felt his hopes rise, and he grabbed the opportunity to ask, "Then you wouldn't advise Macho and me to do it?"

Macho shot Josh a disapproving look, but Thad only laughed. Turning serious, he cautioned, "Absolutely not! You boys need years of diving in safe places before you even think of diving to the sub."

"But it'll be gone by then!" Macho protested. "The Navy's planning to raise the sub and take it so far out in deep water that nobody can dive to it again!"

"That'd suit me, boys! I almost lost my life in that old submarine!"

"Oh?" Josh said, his interest keen. "Tell us about it!"

"Some other time, maybe. The shop's filling up with

customers, so you boys will have to excuse me for now."

As the boys walked outside past a policeman putting a parking ticket on a car's windshield, Josh stopped in surprise. "Hey, look!" he said. "There's Igor!"

"He's just walking by on the other side of the street," Macho responded nonchalantly. "Why're you so nervous about him?"

"Maybe he was watching us—me, I mean. I wonder if he's got a suspicion that I—" Josh dropped his voice and glanced around nervously—"you know."

"You're starting to jump at shadows, Josh! Come on! Let's go meet your mother, and then let's go windsurfing* when we get back to the condos."

Windsurfing appealed to Josh a lot more than diving to the *Bluegill*. So when they had returned to Maalaea Bay,* the boys rented sailboards from a small shop.

"You boys need any pointers on handling these?" the operator asked.

"You kidding?" Macho exclaimed. "We're practically champions!"

"I have to ask," the operator said with a shrug. "We call this the windsurfing capital of the world, so naturally some hot dogs come in, take a few lessons, then decide they're experts.

"But when they get out on the water, some get tired, fall off, and don't have the strength to raise the sail to get back to shore. Sometimes the Coast Guard has to be called out to rescue them, but usually a surfboarder comes by and helps them to shore. You boys be careful."

A little while later, Josh's rainbow-colored sail caught the winds and skittered his board across the bay at an amazing speed. Macho, maneuvering a bright red sail, whooped with joy as his board also slipped across the vast, open expanses of bay.

"Whooee!" Macho called. "We should have brought our fishing line and trolled a lure behind us."

"You kidding? Fish while windsurfing?"

"Lots of guys do it! Hey, look! A porpoise!"

The boys turned to look behind them. Two of the graceful sea animals shot through the air in a circular motion, following the slight wake of the boards.

Josh barely glimpsed the porpoises diving back into the bay before he lost his balance and fell off the board. Macho swept by, laughing at Josh in the water.

Josh recovered, righted the sail, and chased after Macho. They wanted to go see the naval ships anchored beyond Molokini and Kahoolawe, but they knew better. They did sail past the two islands, however, and found themselves outside the bay and on the open sea.

At about the same time, Josh realized he was very tired. He fell off his board more often and found it increasingly difficult to regain his balance. He was comforted by the realization that Macho was having the same probem.

"Hey, Macho," he called, "it's getting on toward sunset, and we're a long way from shore. It'll be dark soon. Maybe we'd better head back."

"No way!" Macho yelled back. "This is too much fun!" He lay panting across his board, the red sail dragging heavily in the water.

Reluctantly, Josh nodded and tried to regain his footing on the board while pulling himself and the sail from the water. It was surprisingly difficult, and Josh gave up, panting hard. He lay on the board, his arm muscles quivering, and glanced around. Shore was a long way off.

"I think the winds changed or something," Josh shouted. "Have you noticed we've been going farther and farther out to sea?"

Macho glanced around so fast that Josh was startled. He saw Macho's face lose color and his eyes widen.

"What's the matter?" Josh asked in alarm.

"The tide! We're caught in the Polynesian Express! It's carrying us out to sea! We may not see land again for a thousand miles—if ever!"

Chapter Six

THE LONGEST NIGHT

Night fell quickly. On his sailboard far out at sea, Josh saw the moon rise over Haleakala's* great, volcanic bulk. The moon paved a shimmering, silver path across the water.

The boys had lashed their masts together with the web belt from Josh's swimming trunks so they wouldn't drift apart. Both sails dragged heavily in the water.

Josh tried to say a prayer, but he couldn't. He felt God couldn't be too happy with him for what he'd been doing, and the sense of not feeling free to ask for God's help doubled his fear. He stretched out on his board, his head on his left forearm. It ached, along with the rest of his upper body, from fruitless paddling toward a shore that had steadily slid away, taking hope with it.

Josh had withdrawn his feet and other arm from the water as well. He didn't expect any sharks to attack, but he'd heard that arms dangling from a board might look like a sea turtle's flippers to an underwater predator. Local divers had told Josh they had often seen the huge turtles minus a flipper or two, proving that sharks enjoy such meals. Josh didn't want to be mistaken for one of the slow-moving turtles.

"Macho?" he called softly into the night.

"What?" Macho did not raise his head from where it rested on his hands.

"You think they'll be looking for us by now?"

"My folks won't, because they don't know where I went."

"Mine know, but they'd never think to look out on the open sea. I figured we'd just play around in the bay."

"Maybe somebody saw us and notified the Coast Guard," Macho said hopefully.

"Let's hope so," Josh replied without much confidence. He raised his head wearily and looked around. The sea was a terribly lonely place. There was no light except the moon. The waves were only about two feet high, barely breaking into whitecaps. "How far you think we've drifted?" he asked.

"I don't know. Miles, anyway." After a pause, Macho added, "I once knew two brothers who were scuba diving with their father when the tide caught them. They couldn't get back to their boat."

Josh didn't answer but listened, trying to conserve what strength remained in his aching body.

"They drifted nine hours and about fifteen miles before they could get back to shore," Macho continued.

Josh shivered, although the night was pleasant and there

was no wind. "My dad would ground me for a million years if I was gone that long," he said.

Macho didn't seem to hear but went on, "My friends were being swept along the coastline, but you and I are well out to sea. I can't see a single light anywhere, not even from the naval ships searching for that sunken sub. Guess it was like that when my three friends got in trouble. Only they had a problem before reaching shore."

Josh didn't want to talk about that, but he knew there was no choice. "Oh?" he prompted grudgingly.

"In the night, after dropping their tanks and everything except their fins, these two guys and their father were floating along on their backs. They knew enough not to fight the current, so they were saving their strength when...." Macho's voice trailed off.

"When what?" Josh asked, feeling he really shouldn't have.

"When they saw two shark fins circling them."

Josh's eyes flickered rapidly around the dark ocean. He half expected to see a dorsal fin slicing through the water toward him. Finally he asked, "What happened then?"

"It was a moonlit night like this, so they could see the tips of the fins. They stuck about two and a half feet out of the water."

"Sounds like mighty big sharks."

"They figured the sharks were about ten to twelve feet long, either oceanic white tips or tiger sharks. They couldn't be sure."

"So what did they do?" Josh asked, his curiosity piqued.

"The sharks circled several times. My friends turned with them, always facing them."

Josh nodded, remembering he had done that with the tiger that took Macho's fish on the stringer.

"The sharks kept coming closer. Then one made a pass right between the father and his older son."

Again, Josh didn't want to ask, but he had to know: "What-what happened?"

"The shark bumped the older brother. He said the shark's skin felt like fine-grade sandpaper—not really coarse, but tough. The father and other brother saw the shark do that. They naturally thought the boy had been hit, but he was okay. Then both sharks disappeared."

Josh was silent a moment, thinking. Then he asked, "Why'd you tell me that story?"

Macho's white teeth flashed in the moonlight as he replied, "To see if it scared you."

It had, but Josh didn't admit that. Instead, his eyes skimmed the sea in fearful anticipation of seeing dorsal fins slicing the water toward him. Then he tried to look under the board, but it was too dark to see more than a foot or so beneath the surface. If one of the great beasts struck from below, there would be no warning.

"Macho!" Josh pushed his upper body up suddenly, straining to see into the night. "Look! Isn't that a light?"

The older boy swiveled his head the way Josh was looking. "Sure is! Hey! The tide's changed! That's a point of land! We're being carried toward shore!"

Forgetting the risk of looking like sea turtles' flippers from below, both boys began paddling with their hands. But Josh quickly realized there was no forward progress.

"The sails!" he puffed. "They're dragging so deep in the water we can't move! Let's see if we can unfasten them. Dump them overboard!"

Tired as they were, the boys seemed all thumbs and no fingers, but eventually both sails fell free.

"Now," Macho said, "let's paddle straight for that light!"

It seemed to take forever, but with the aid of a strong inbound tide, the boys finally reached shore. They staggered onto the beach a few feet and collapsed.

"We made it!" Macho said with a weary laugh.

"Thank God for that!" Josh said. "Let's rest and then try to find a phone. Boy, is my father going to be mad!"

"Tell him he's lucky to have a living son return to him," Macho suggested. "Then maybe he won't be so hard on you."

Macho was only partly right. When a police car delivered the boys to their condos shortly before dawn, Josh's parents engulfed him in joyful embraces. But that soon passed. Josh saw by the look on his father's face that he was very upset.

Uh-oh, Josh told himself, *here it comes!*

Josh's mother led Tiffany and Nathan out onto the

lanai* and closed the sliding glass door. Mr. Ladd took Josh into the boys' room and closed the door and window.

"Sit down, Son," he said.

Josh sat gingerly on the edge of his twin bed. The jaw muscle twitched in his father's somber face. When the man spoke, his voice was tightly controlled and barely audible. "Son, your mother and I—with your sister and brother—have just spent the most miserable hours of our lives, wondering where you were."

"I'm sorry, Dad." Josh's voice was low, his head down.

"We prayed for your safety. We called Pastor Chin back in Honolulu and asked him to get the church's prayer chain going for you. We called every emergency authority we could think of: police, Coast Guard and hospitals. Nathan even suggested calling the morgue."

Josh didn't reply, although he wasn't surprised his little brother had thought of such a gruesome thing.

"Son, these anguished hours gave your mother and me some time to think about your new friend, Macho. You've never brought him over so we could *both* meet him and talk to him, and that's against our family rules. We insist on knowing your friends. I'm sorry I failed to enforce that rule."

"I'll bring him over later today, Dad."

"Thank you. While we fretted tonight, wondering where you were and whether you were alive or dead, we naturally talked to Macho's mother. His father wasn't home. Frankly, I was surprised Mrs. Langford didn't seem very concerned about the boy. She said he often stays out quite late. I can't conceive of such an attitude, but I know some parents are like that."

Josh didn't say anything. His father continued, "Your mother and I also talked with Tank."

"What'd he tell you?" Josh asked, looking up quickly.

"Only that you and he had a disagreement over Macho and that the two of you aren't speaking."

"Oh," Josh said in a low, relieved voice.

His father's parental sense that something was being hidden from him made him ask sharply, "Why did you ask? Is there something you should tell me?"

Josh wanted to say yes and tell the whole story, but he kept still. *If I tell him,* he thought, *all our lives could be in danger! But if I don't tell, I'll be lying to my father, and that's very wrong.*

"I'm waiting for your answer, Son," Mr. Ladd said crisply.

"I—I—"

"Look at me!"

Slowly, the boy raised his face, but he couldn't meet his father's eyes. Sadly he said, "I can't tell you, Dad."

"Can't—or won't?"

"Can't!" Josh shouted, jumping up, his blue eyes pleading with his father's. "Oh, Dad, I *want* to tell you, but I just can't!"

Mr. Ladd was silent a long moment, his eyes probing deep into his son's. Finally he said softly, "I see. I take it that this isn't some minor situation, but something of extreme importance to you."

"Yes, and to all our family, too! Oh, Dad! Please don't ask me, but believe me, it's a matter of life and death!"

His father reached out and pulled the boy to him. Loving arms encircled Josh like a strong, protective band. "I have mixed feelings, Son," he said. "I don't think whatever you're burdened with is as critical as you do. I also don't understand why you think you can't tell me about it.

"However," he continued, "I respect your belief that you're doing something very dangerous. Still, I can't rest until I find out what terrible danger you imagine we're in because of some boyish secret."

Josh jerked his head back and looked up at his father, fighting tears. "It's not a boyish secret!" Josh insisted. "It's a terrible one! And I don't *imagine* we're in danger—I *know* we are if I don't keep quiet!"

There was a long silence while Mr. Ladd looked into his son's anguished face and thought about what Josh had said. Finally he said, "I see, Son. Well, I'm going to talk with your mother about what to do. We'll withhold final judgment on your friendship with Macho until we have more information. In the meantime, you'd better stick pretty close to the condo. Oh, and of course you'll have to pay out of your own allowance for that sail you dumped in the ocean."

Overwhelmed by his dad's obvious love and concern,

Josh felt hot tears seep out of the corners of his eyes. That made him mad, because he considered himself too old to cry. "Thanks," he whispered.

His father gave him another quick hug and left the room in silence. When the door had closed, Josh sniffed loudly and tried to gain control of his emotions. "Oh, Lord! I'm so mixed up!" he whispered. "I don't know what to do. Please help me."

Josh lowered his face. Through a scalding mist of unwanted tears, he saw the corner of the chest of drawers had been pulled away from the wall.

If Nathan— Josh thought, anger surging through him like a hot wave. Quickly he pulled the chest back and glanced at the videotape. *Still there! He didn't find it—or did he?*

Josh reached around and carefully felt the transparent tape he'd used to hold the case in place. *Seems okay,* he decided, *but how I wish I didn't have to keep hiding this thing!*

Later that morning, after Josh had slept fitfully for just a few hours, he stepped out on the lanai for a look around. Strangely, the bay was empty of the usual fishing boats and sight-seeing catamarans* heading for Molokini.* *Something's up,* he told himself. *Maybe the Coast Guard or Navy isn't letting them go out. But the naval ships are still out there where I saw—*

He broke off the thought when he saw Macho walking the narrow strip of sandy beach, looking up at mynah* birds in the palm trees. Josh turned and hurried out the front door and down the outside stairs.

"Hey, Macho!" he called half a minute later, trotting up to the other boy. "What'd your mother say when you got home?"

"Not much. She was most upset that your folks came charging over in the middle of the night. What'd your parents do to you?"

"Nothing yet. But you can be sure they will, and soon. Meanwhile, my dad wants to meet you."

"I figured as much. Well, let's get it over with."

Josh frowned at the expression, but he took Macho upstairs. There he introduced him to his father, then sat back and listened.

Mr. and Mrs. Ladd were polite, but Josh could see they were carefully evaluating Macho. After the brief meeting, Josh and Macho took the elevator downstairs.

"Your mom was nice the other day, and your dad seems okay, too," Macho said.

Josh thought there was a hint of sadness or maybe even envy in Macho's voice. "They're the best, Macho," he replied.

Macho's tone hardened as he said, "You're just saying that because your old man didn't ground you for last night."

"Don't call him that," Josh replied, flinching at the disrespectful reference to his father.

"He and your mom were sure looking me over," Macho

said with a shrug. "Asking all those questions and every-thing. Who'd they think I am, some kind of monster in a boy's body?"

"They're trying to be fair, that's all! They've never ac-tually forbidden me to spend time with any kids, but they sure have discouraged me from hanging out with some."

"Like me?"

"They're still deciding."

The elevator door slid open, and the boys walked out into the parking lot. "Speaking of deciding," Macho said, "when're we going to dive down to the *Bluegill*?"

Josh shook his head hard. "After last night, I'm not doing anything that's dangerous!"

"We only went windsurfing! What happened could have happened to anybody!"

"Maybe, but I'm already in enough trouble with my parents without diving to that sub after they told me I couldn't."

"Speaking of subs, did you hear the news this morning about the search for that Soviet sub?"

"Shh!" Josh grabbed the other boy's arm hard and glanced around. No one was near, but Josh's heart had leaped into a scared gallop. "Don't ever say anything like that in public again!"

"Don't get so uptight! Nobody heard. Anyway, there's a Russian trawler reported off Maui, just like we read about when the first sub sank years ago."

"As long as they stay in the ocean, I don't care."

"They've got to have spies on land, too, trying to help pinpoint the sub's exact location. Say, you know what?"

Josh didn't like the way Macho was grinning. "What?" he asked cautiously.

"What if I said you dive with me to the *Bluegill* or I tell your secret to someone?"

Josh stopped stock-still, the color draining from his face. "You wouldn't!" he said, overcoming his shock. "You promised!"

"Don't get so upset," Macho said with a smile. "It was just a question."

"It was a terrible question! Like blackmail! And this is the second time you've done that! But you can't break your word any more than I can!"

"Forget it, Josh! Now, let's talk about when we make that dive to the *Bluegill*."

In that instant, something changed between Josh and Macho. Josh didn't know if the other boy was joking about revealing the secret. But because of the way Macho had said it, immediately followed by the positive statement that the boys were going to make the dangerous dive, Josh was suddenly afraid in a way he'd never been in his life.

It's only a matter of time, Josh told himself, *and then I've got to make that dive, no matter what Mom and Dad say, or maybe he* will *tell.*

Josh didn't want to make the dive, didn't want to at all. He had a very bad feeling about it. But he couldn't see any other choice at the moment.

Chapter Seven

WHO'S A SPY?

After hearing Macho's not-too-subtle threat, Josh was glad he had to stay close to the condo until his parents decided how to discipline him over the windsurfing incident. He really wanted to be alone to think. So when he had excused himself, he made his way to his bedroom.

Once there, Josh changed into his bathing suit. As he came out carrying a beach towel, he saw his father standing on the lanai* and holding binoculars to his eyes.

John Ladd lowered the glasses and turned to his older son. "Those Navy ships are still on station beyond Molokini* and Kahoolawe,*" he said. "I don't see any fishing or tourist vessels anchored against the protected inside curve of Molokini. Must have something to do with that missing Soviet sub."

Josh tried to keep his face from showing he knew anything. *If there are Soviet spies around,* he thought, *they've seen all that activity. Maybe they've guessed what it means. But what can they do about it?*

Aloud he asked, "What's the latest news on the Soviet ships reported heading this way?"

"Still coming, the last I heard."

"Do you think they're heading for the same place?" He motioned toward the anchored American naval vessels.

"Maybe, but I don't think either country wants a direct confrontation. Not even if the missing sub is what's out there."

"What do you think will happen?"

"My guess is that the Soviets would try to destroy what's left of their sub. I mean, before our people can recover its guidance system or whatever other secrets it has."

"How could they do that?"

"Not being a military person, I can't even guess. But I'm positive the sub's secrets are now the prize in a race between the two superpowers. So if something goes wrong, or the stakes are big enough, well—I just hope it doesn't escalate into some kind of military action."

Josh's voice was a hoarse, frightened whisper. "You mean—shooting and killing?"

"I hope not, Son."

Josh's thoughts rolled and tumbled as he walked to the elevator. *If our guys have found the sub, I should feel safe. But if Dad's right, I've still got to keep the secret until there's no chance it can be blown up. Otherwise, if Soviet agents found out that I have the exact location and forced it out of me, maybe they could reach the sub before our navy has a chance to recover the things it wants from it.*

Feeling miserable and uncertain, Josh rode from the fourth floor down to the second, where the elevator stopped. Josh was staring at his feet, lost in thought, and didn't notice as the door opened and Igor got on.

"Must talk!" Igor said.

Startled, Josh looked up. The instant he realized what was happening, he darted toward the closing door, but Igor blocked the way. The grim-faced man stood silently looking down at the boy as the door shut and the elevator started moving again.

Suddenly, Igor reached over and pulled out the red emergency stop button. The elevator jerked to a halt between floors.

"Hey," Josh cried, "what're you doing?"

"Must talk!" Igor repeated.

Josh leaped forward and pushed the button back in, sending the elevator on its way again. He blocked Igor's arm with his own as the man grasped for the control panel. Soon the elevator stopped at the ground floor, and Josh ducked under Igor's arms and ran hard toward the beach.

It took Josh a few minutes to calm his racing heart. *If I tell Dad that Igor's bothering me,* he thought, *Dad'll want to know why. And since I can't tell him that, I'll have to deal with Igor by myself, too.*

Josh spread out his towel on the plastic lounge chair, figuring Igor wouldn't try to corner him in public. Then

he turned his thoughts to Macho. *Would he really
break his promise?* Josh sat in the shade of a coconut palm
and stared moodily out over the water. *He's forcing me
to make that dive to the* Bluegill *by threatening me. He
pretended it was only a joke, but I think he really meant it.*

Sensing a movement beside him, Josh looked up. Nancy Hogan, in her fluorescent bathing suit, smiled down
on him. She pointed to a nearby, empty lounge chair and
asked, "May I?"

Josh nodded, and she sat down, still smiling. "A friend
of mine just got in from the Mainland," she said. "I'd
like you to meet him."

"I'm always glad to meet people."

"Thanks, Josh. You'll like him." Nancy turned and
waved toward the swimming pool. "Jack," she called in
a soft voice that still carried the forty feet to the pool,
"come meet the young friend I was telling you about."

Josh got to his feet as the tall, muscular man in bright
orange swim trunks and zoris* approached.

"Jack Simms, meet Josh Ladd," Nancy said.

The big man flashed a friendly grin and gripped Josh's
right hand in a strong handshake. "A pleasure, Josh!" he
said. "Nancy tells me you've been very nice to her since
she arrived."

Josh shrugged as all three sat down. Jack and Nancy
sandwiched the boy between them.

"I heard through the coconut wireless* that you and
Macho had quite an experience while windsurfing,"

Nancy prompted.

Josh didn't want to talk about his sailboarding adventure. Nancy sensed his discomfort and flashed a warm smile as she said, "Oh, I'm sorry! I should have realized that experience could be a sensitive subject for you. Forgive me, Josh, please!"

"It's okay," he replied, looking across the bay to the naval ships anchored there.

"You like to dive, Josh?" Jack asked.

"Some. My friend Tank—" Josh's voice broke at the automatic reference to his estranged friend. He continued, "My friends and I do lots of snorkeling and a little skin diving. We recently got our Junior Open Water Diver Certification so we can do scuba diving, too."

"Have you made your first scuba dive yet?" Jack asked, spreading sunscreen lotion on his legs.

"Yeah, I've made a few shallow dives, but—" Josh hesitated a moment, knowing what he wanted to say was meant to impress Nancy and Jack—"but I'm thinking of going down to explore that old World War II submarine the Navy sank in Lahaina* Harbor some years back."

The moment he said it, Josh was sorry. *I'm beginning to sound like Macho!* he scolded himself.

"Oh, my!" Nancy exclaimed, reaching over to touch Josh's arm. "I hope you won't do anything like that! It's surely very dangerous!"

Josh started to answer just as his sister leaned over the lanai railing and called, "Josh, Mom wants us all to go to the store with her!"

The boy excused himself and went upstairs to change into shorts and tee shirt. He didn't enjoy shopping with his mother, sister and little brother. But since he was on probation with his parents, he couldn't take any chances of making things worse by complaining. He also suspected his mother hadn't suggested the shopping trip lightly. She had something else on her mind.

Mary Ladd talked of casual things as she drove around the east end of the bay toward the small town of Kihei.* When they reached the supermarket and went in, Josh got a shopping cart and pushed it for his mother. Tiffany and Nathan walked well ahead down the aisles.

Josh's mother picked up a plastic package with orange-red contents and dropped it in the wire basket. "Are you and Tank speaking, Josh?" she asked.

Josh recognized the food item as what the local Japanese called *tako**—octopus. He didn't like the taste or feel of the rubbery little creatures. He especially didn't like the countless tiny suction cups on their eight legs. But the rest of his family liked the Hawaiian delicacy, so it was often served at dinner.

"Sorta," Josh answered his mother's question. He watched a small English sparrow picking at some crumbs on the grocery store floor. It was at least two hundred feet from the open front door. The bird flew up behind a bank of fluorescent lights to finish eating.

"You two've been friends since you were babies," his

mother reminded him. It was a leading statement, Josh knew. She wanted him to answer.

"We had a disagreement about Macho."

"So your father told me. Do you want to talk about it?"

"Not really."

Tiffany returned in time to hear his answer. She shot him a big-sister look of disapproval and whispered under her breath, "Not smart, Josh! Not smart at all!"

"Leave me alone!" he growled, glaring at her.

"I see," Mrs. Ladd said softly, picking up a package of fresh ono.* "Well, Joshua, when you're ready...."

She let the sentence trail off. Josh winced, knowing that when she called him by his full name, she was displeased.

"Hey!" Nathan exclaimed, coming back to the cart. "There's Tank and that guy with the funny way of talking."

"Igor Petrov," Mary Ladd said, following her younger son's pointing hand. "He speaks with an accent because he was born in Russia. I've explained that to you before, Nathan. Please try to remember."

"Bet he's a spy!" Nathan whispered. "He's a spy for all those Russian ships looking for the sub that sank!"

"Nathan!" His mother's voice was crisp. "Don't ever say that again! Just because he speaks with an accent is no reason to suspect him of anything like that! In fact, it's a good reason *not* to suspect him! From what I've read and your father says, an intelligence agent wouldn't be so obvious."

Josh wasn't convinced, especially in light of the way

Igor kept trying to get him alone to talk to him. He watched Tank and Igor in thoughtful silence.

Nathan muttered under his breath, "Bet he is too a spy!"

When Igor walked out of the store and Tank began looking at something in a glass case, Mary Ladd suggested, "Josh, now's a good time to patch things up with Tank."

Josh thought about that a moment, then nodded. He missed his friend very much.

As Josh approached, Tank looked up. His face started to brighten in the usual welcome, but then it faded into an impassive mask.

Josh looked into the case where cameras and tape recorders were displayed, avoiding Tank's eyes. "I don't know how to say this," Josh began, "but, well—" He hesitated, his sentence unfinished.

"You trying to say you're sorry?" Tank suggested.

Josh started to nod, then stopped. He was so anxious that he felt he had to ask, "What were you and Igor talking about just now?"

"You're still thinking maybe I told about you know what, aren't you?" Tank said with an edge in his voice.

"I was just asking!" Josh exclaimed. He felt the opportunity to make up with Tank start to slip away.

"I wouldn't betray a friend—or a *former* friend, either! But it makes me mad that you'd even think I would!"

"No need to get angry," Josh protested, glancing around to make sure nobody else was listening.

Tank's eyes were bright with pain and anger. "*I* wouldn't tell a friend's secret," he continued, "but I'm not so sure about your new friend Macho!"

Josh wanted to explain about Macho's threats and why he had to stay friends with him, but he checked himself, stung by Tank's reaction. Instead he blurted, "Oh, yeah? Well, you don't have to worry about him! And you don't have to make nasty suggestions about him, either!"

"What's gotten into you lately, Josh?" Tank asked. "You and I were always adventuresome, but we were never reckless like you were on that windsurfer."

Josh didn't mean to, but he felt himself getting defensive and angry. "You saying I'm reckless?" he challenged.

Tank's voice rose slightly and became harder. "I'm saying that lately you're not the same Josh Ladd I've known all my life!"

"Well, maybe I'm just growing up! Maybe I'm ready to go past adventures little kids have! I'm having some grown-up ones!"

"Like what?"

"Like—like diving with Macho onto the *Bluegill*!"

Josh almost bit his tongue at what he'd said. He didn't mean it—not a word of it. Yet it had somehow exploded into the conversation.

Tank looked sadly at Josh and slowly shook his head as he said, "I don't think you'd do anything as foolish as that!"

Josh started to make another angry reply, but instead

he abruptly turned away and stormed out of the store.

Now, why'd I do that? Josh asked himself as soon as he was outside. *Things are getting worse and worse!*

Just then, Macho came running out of a nearby shop. "Hey, Josh!" he called. "Great news!"

"What?"

"I know a couple of men who're going down to the *Bluegill* tomorrow, and they said we can dive with them!"

Chapter Eight

DIVE TO DANGER

Josh heard alarm bells going off inside his head as Macho stopped in front of him, white teeth gleaming in a broad smile. "We're going to dive on the *Bluegill* tomorrow?" Josh said.

"Yeah! Isn't that fabulous?"

"Uh, yeah!"

"You don't seem very enthusiastic."

"Well, I, uh, hadn't expected it so soon, so you sorta took me by surprise."

"Good thing it's coming up fast! Otherwise your parents might ground you over the windsurfing thing. Then we'd never get to make the dive."

"Well, actually," Josh said, thinking fast, "they already told me I couldn't make the dive on the *Bluegill*, so—"

"You nuts?" Macho interrupted. "Are you going to miss a chance like this just because of your parents? The thing to do is keep your mouth shut and just do it!"

"Uh, Macho, I just can't—"

"Aren't you forgetting something?" Macho cut in again,

his voice hard and his eyes narrowed. "If you don't dive with me, I might tell your secret. Then you and your folks would be in deep trouble!"

"That's about the third time—"

"Just kidding, of course!" With a smile he added, "We'll go exploring inside the *Bluegill*—"

"Inside?" Josh broke in, his voice rising in alarm. "I thought we were just going to dive to the outside!"

"That wouldn't be any fun! Oops! Your mother's coming out of the store! You'd better go before she sees us together. Otherwise, she might not let you go. See you in the morning!"

Josh stood there, frustration and anger flooding over him. *Macho always tries to make a joke out of his threats,* he thought, *but I think they're real. He's manipulating me, but what can I do about it?*

On the way back to the condo in the back seat of his mother's rental sedan, Josh was unusually quiet. His mother turned down the radio and looked at her son in the rearview mirror. "You all right, Josh?" she asked.

"Huh? Oh, yeah, sure. Would you mind turning up the radio again, Mom? I was listening to the news."

"Nothing new," she replied. "The CIA's saying it hasn't been able to locate the Russian submarine."

Josh shook his head. "In the old newspaper stories about the first sub, they didn't admit finding it until much later. Then they claimed it broke in two and they only recovered part of it."

Nathan, sitting beside Josh in the back seat, said with all the confidence of his ten years, "Everybody knows that spies make up cover stories.*"

From the front passenger seat, Tiffany said, "I sure hope our guys find that robot sub before the Russians do!"

"I guess it's hard being in a branch of government where truth is a stranger," Mary Ladd commented. "But I guess that's the only way they feel our country can be protected from potential enemies. Still, I don't like deceit of any kind."

Josh licked his lips, guilt seeping over him again. He said quickly, "Well, they'd have to be careful, because they'd surely know that reporters would go back to the old files and review what happened after the first sub sank."

"I suppose I'm naive," his mother said with a sigh, "but I really don't know much about intelligence operations."

"You mean spies?" Nathan asked, leaning forward eagerly. "I can tell you. I see all the television programs about spies."

Josh smiled and rumpled his brother's hair. "I just wish you were half as smart about such things as you think you are! I'd rent you out to the Navy, and you could solve all their problems without having to find that sub that sank off Kahoolawe.*"

Tiffany twisted around in her seat to face Josh. "Where'd you hear it sank off Kahoolawe?" she demanded.

Josh swallowed hard, realizing he'd made a slip. "Uh, why else would all those ships be anchored there? Like Dad said earlier today, they must be part of the search for the sub."

Then he kicked himself, thinking, *There's another little white lie! Well, it wasn't really a lie, I guess. But I misled her, and that's like a lie. They keep growing!*

Mrs. Ladd again studied her older son in the mirror. "Earlier," she said with a hint of suspiciousness, "the news said those ships were exploring for some kind of valuable mineral on the ocean floor."

"Manganese nodules," Josh explained. "That's what the government announced it was doing years ago when it was looking for that first Soviet sub. It's in those photocopies of old newspapers I brought home from the library. But that's not really something the Navy would do, you know. That kind of exploration is done by commercial companies."

"That must have been on the missing page you couldn't find," Tiffany said. "At least, I didn't read that part."

Josh frowned, thinking, *Where did that paper go? I know I copied it.*

"What's magnesia?" Nathan asked.

"Manganese," Tiffany corrected her little brother. "I studied that in chemistry. It's a kind of metallic element used in making steel tough."

Josh's mother looked at him in the mirror again. He dropped his eyes. "Still, you seem very sure about why all those ships are there," she said.

Josh turned to stare blankly out the window at the acres of sugarcane on both sides of the road. The long, narrow plants were bending over hard, whipped by stiff winds.

Got to watch it! he warned himself. *She's suspicious. But she trusts me—and that makes me feel even more miserable!*

The rest of the trip was made without incident, but as they waited for the elevator back at the condo, Josh's mother exclaimed, "Oh, I forgot dishwashing detergent! I'm completely out, too. Josh, please run down to the little store and get the smallest box you can."

Josh was glad to have some time alone to think about the mountain of troubles piling up around him. He took the money his mother offered and headed toward the wharf where the convenience store was located.

How am I going to keep from diving down inside that sub tomorrow? he asked himself as he passed the be-still and ironwood trees. *We could get the bends or cut our air hoses on an old pipe or something!*

"I been vaiting for you." The words came softly from an open car window as Josh passed a line of three dust-covered cars under an overhanging be-still tree. Josh recognized Igor Petrov's accent even before the man opened the car door and stepped out fast, blocking Josh's way.

"Uh, I'm in a hurry," Josh said desperately. "Got to get to the store right away."

Igor frowned, his heavy eyebrows settling down like great blackbird's wings. He stood menacingly, with legs apart and hands on hips. "Alvays in hurry!" he said. "Vy you no talk to me, huh?"

Josh dodged around the man as he answered, "My mom—"

"Vy you von't talk vit' me?" Igor interrupted with controlled anger, swinging into step with the hurrying boy. "Vy ever'one look at me funny ven I valk by and dey talk about submarine sunk? You t'ink I spy, da?"

"Uh," Josh began, knowing he couldn't admit Igor was right. Josh wasn't used to hiding things or being dishonest. But then, neither was he used to feeling his family was in danger because of something only he knew.

"Da?" Igor asked again, matching Josh's stride as he started to jog.

"I really can't talk now!" Josh cried, breaking into a hard run. "Sorry!" With that, he sprinted off.

"You *vill* be sorry!" Igor called, but Josh didn't look back until he turned seaward toward the convenience store.

Josh made his purchase, then decided to walk back to the condo by way of the beach in case Igor were still waiting for him on the roadway. As he walked along he wondered, *He must have heard about the tape and that I know where the sub is. Why else would he insist on talking to me? But how did he find out? Only Tank and Macho knew! What if Igor becomes dangerous?*

The boy spent a miserable evening. Before dinner, his father put on the silver-framed half-glasses he'd recently started wearing for reading. He scanned the front page of the day's newspaper, then looked across the top of it at Josh.

"Your mother told me about your theory that the Navy is looking for the sunken sub off Kahoolawe, Son," he began. "I've been wondering why they're out there, too, as you know. But there's nothing in the paper or on television about that. The ships aren't doing anything unusual that I can see, either. Do you have any particular reason for thinking that's why they're there?"

Josh knew he had to answer his father carefully. "Maybe their listening devices gave them the general location of the explosion, but they're not able to find the wreck yet."

"Makes sense," his father agreed.

"Or maybe they're waiting for a special ship to come help with the salvage," Josh added. "That's what was done with the first sub."

"Yes, I remember seeing pictures in those old newspaper clips you brought home. Had tonglike claws that apparently grabbed at least part of the Russian sub— maybe all of it."

"Do you really think that's what's going on out there, Dear?" Mary Ladd asked.

"It's possible, I suppose. But we may never know for sure, unless the Soviets get to the wreck first and blow it up."

"Blow it up?" Mrs. Ladd exclaimed.

"What else can they do? They can't salvage it under the very noses of those naval gunships."

Josh got up suddenly and walked out onto the lanai,* too upset to join in more conversation. He stared out over the bay. Thoughts tumbled over one another in such rapid succession that he couldn't separate them clearly.

Could we get into a shoot-out with the Russians because of what I know? What's Igor going to do to me? What's going to happen if I dive down to the Bluegill *with Macho? I should tell my parents everything, but they'll go to the police or somebody. Then it'd leak to Russian spies, and everybody will be in danger: Dad, Mom, Tiffany, Nathan—and me!*

After dinner, the family took turns reading the Bible and praying. When it came his turn, Josh barely mumbled the words of Scripture. He didn't pray at all, which caused all the other family members to look at him strangely.

The next morning, Josh slipped away shortly after breakfast to join Macho in the parking lot. Josh was miserable inside. *I'm afraid*, he admitted to himself as he and Macho climbed into the back of a pickup truck with two men in the cab. *Afraid of the dive. Afraid of what my folks will say when they learn I've disobeyed. Afraid of what Macho will do if I don't make the dive with him. I never used to have to worry about things like this!*

As the men and boys suited up at a small beach near

Lahaina,* Josh immediately sensed that both men were grown-up versions of Macho. They bragged loudly of their skill and daring.

When everyone was in full scuba gear, the men untied a small outboard motorboat at the water's edge. All four people scrambled in, and the boat headed out to where the *Bluegill* rested on a sandy bottom. Josh's nerves were on edge from the constant stream of bragging from the two men and Macho.

Well, let them talk! Josh thought crossly. *I'll save my breath for the dive.* He barely noticed the sting of salt spray on his face as he watched the island of Lanai ahead and slightly off to the right, with Kahoolawe to the left.

Josh's father had told him about this harbor, or roadstead. A century and a half ago, hundreds of whaling ships anchored here. When the rough whalers went ashore, they often had conflicts with American missionaries who were bringing the gospel to native Hawaiians.

The motor died, and the anchor was tossed overboard. Josh watched it fall down, down to catch on the *Bluegill*'s superstructure. Hawaii's blue waters still amazed Josh. He could see clearly the 311-foot-long submarine 135 feet down.

"Isn't she a beaut?" asked the tall man who had steered the boat. "Looks like a gigantic whale, except for the conning tower and the hatches."

"Sure is a sight!" Macho agreed. "Huh, Josh?"

Josh stared in horrified fascination at the long, cigar-shaped hulk waiting below. "Never saw anything like it—uh, quite like it," he added, remembering the stricken Soviet robot sub.

"Well," Macho said, "let's go down and see what she's like inside."

The two men and Macho entered the water. Josh followed, not wanting to risk his life foolishly but seeing no way out of the situation.

The first man started to adjust his regulator over his mouth but stopped, looking at his buddy in alarm. "Andy, what's the matter?" he said.

Josh blinked in surprise at the other man. He was breathing fast and hard, making strange rasping sounds.

The first man examined his friend, then exclaimed, "He's hyperventilating!"

"What's that mean?" Macho asked.

"It means he's breathing too fast and too deep because he's scared," the man answered. "That causes a decrease of carbon dioxide in the blood. He can't dive like this, and I won't go down without him!"

For a moment, Josh felt a sense of great relief. If the men couldn't dive, surely neither could he and Macho! "Is he going to be all right?" Josh asked.

"Oh, sure! It's no sin to be scared of a dive like this, you know. He'll be okay in a minute, but we can't risk having him do that down there. Our dive's off."

Josh wanted to cheer, but Macho spoiled his joy. "Any

reason you two can't wait here while Josh and I go down?" he asked.

Josh wanted to shout "Yes!" but the taller man shrugged and answered, "If you two are dumb enough to try it alone, yeah, Andy and I can wait here for you."

Josh numbly saw his reprieve slipping away, then thought of something else that suddenly renewed his hope. "Where's the safety line?*" he asked.

"I thought you had it!" Macho growled. "And where's the other light?"

Josh sighed inwardly with relief. "Forgot it, I guess," he said. "Well, without a safety line and only one light between us, we'd better call it off, too."

"No way!" Macho insisted. He looked at the two men now back in the boat and said, "Hey, let us borrow your lights and rope."

The taller man shook his head. "Sorry, kids," he answered, "but we don't loan equipment."

Josh started to breathe a sigh of relief again, but Macho muttered, "We're going to make this dive anyway! Come on, Josh!" With that he dived under the surface, leaving Josh feeling he had little choice but to follow.

A moment later, bubbles flowing from his regulator, Josh trailed Macho down toward the sub, black and threatening. It looked like a long tomb waiting to swallow them forever.

Oh, Lord, Josh prayed silently, *what've I done?* He knew he'd soon find out—maybe the hard way!

Chapter Nine

TERROR IN AN OLD SUBMARINE

Small, brightly colored, tropical reef fish flashed about the boys as they began their slow descent. In Hawaii's clear waters, free of the plankton* common to most shores, they could see more than a hundred feet in every direction.

As the boys followed the anchor cable down, they periodically checked their watches and depth gauges. They hadn't planned this dive carefully as they had been taught, and Josh realized this was another foolish decision. Yet shortly after they had passed one hundred feet down, he found his fears fading.

It took Josh a moment to realize nitrogen narcosis was starting to affect him. He'd studied that in earning his diving certificate. Nitrogen is a gas, and *narcosis* means "a state of drowsiness." In a deep dive, it sometimes shows up as a good feeling, but it's dangerous.

Josh remembered his instructor's warnings: "Nitrogen narcosis won't make you want to give your regulator away to a fish. But everything that's interesting is more so, while everything that's picturesque is more so. If you see your diving buddy staring foolishly at his pressure gauge, you know he's being affected by nitrogen narcosis."

Josh wondered if Macho was feeling the same thing. But there was no way of communicating except by hand signals, and Josh didn't know how to signal that question. Instead, he reassured himself that everything was going to be all right by recalling that thousands of safe recreational dives had been made on the *Bluegill*.

We'll be okay, Josh told himself. At once he had to shake off an unpleasant afterthought: *I remember reading that more people have to go through recompression chambers* after this dive than any other dive in the state. Some end up with the bends, too. Mustn't get careless.*

The one light between Josh and Macho became ever more important as they went deeper and gradually left the surface sunlight far above them.

Josh's sense of danger receded steadily. He enjoyed the dive with heightened awareness, forgetting about the foolishness of having only one light, no spare bottle of air and no lifeline. Igor no longer seemed a threat. Macho's recklessness seemed less important. Josh even began to forget about the threat to his family's safety.

The boys explored the outside of the vessel's 311 feet. At the conning tower, Josh's imagination re-created sounds of what it might have been like as the diesel-powered sub prepared to submerge.

"Dive! Dive!"

"Aoogah! Aoogah!" the Klaxon horn sounded.

The boat crash-dived under her own power, waves washing over her decks. The *Bluegill* had sunk 46,000 tons of enemy shipping in World War II. Now she rested where she had been deliberately sunk in Auau Channel* in December 1970.

Macho pointed to an open hatch at the bow.* When he started swimming in that direction, Josh followed. A vague sense of danger began nibbling at the back of his mind again.

Treading water over the open hatch, Macho jabbed his right forefinger downward into the sub's interior. Josh shook his head, but Macho just shrugged and eased through the hatch, taking the only light with him. Josh glanced at his watch and depth gauge, then silently called, *Hey! Wait for me!* as he hurried to stay close.

The sub's interior surprised Josh. The blue water was perfectly clear, just as it had been outside the sub. As Macho flashed the light around, Josh saw there was no surge of tide at this depth. The sub's single open overhead hatch prevented anything from disturbing the water inside. There were no fish, octopi or sea turtles such as an underground cavern or lava tube* would have. The two boys were the only living things aboard.

This is great! Josh thought. He glanced around as Macho moved the light. Looking into the end compartment, he recognized the forward torpedo room. His imagination could again hear echoes from the past.

"Ready all tubes!"

"Tubes ready, Sir."

"Fire one!"

"One fired, Sir."

The sub had been gutted before it was sunk. All that was left of its equipment were countless protruding metal pipes and pieces of steel that could snag a diver's gear. Stalactites* hung down like icicles, and stalagmites* grew up from the deck.

Josh had read what caused these and recalled the information now: *Batteries! The* Bluegill *used its diesel engines for surface running, where the exhaust could be vented. But underwater it used lead-acid batteries for power. Those have gone into suspension, with the sulfur separating out and growing everywhere. The high sulfur content also poisons the water, and that's why nothing lives in here.*

Josh wanted to share all these thoughts with Macho, but there was no way. Instead, he followed his companion's light through one compartment after another.

In the officers' and crews' quarters, drawers had been pulled out and left open by submariners long gone. There had once been laughter and music and conversation here. Josh's imagination kicked in once more.

"I'll sure be glad when this war's over!"

"Me, too! But right now, I'd like to know how my wife and baby are doing. I've never seen him."

"Sing us a song, Dick!"

Swimming side by side, Josh and Macho came to a hatchway directly under the conning tower. Josh estimated they were now a hundred feet or more into the sub's interior.

Macho flashed his light on the hatchway and tried to move it. When he couldn't, Josh tried. He was also unsuccessful. Both boys tried together.

No use! Josh thought, motioning to Macho. *It's dogged down too tight.*

Macho nodded in understanding and started to swim deeper into the silent sub.

Josh reached over and lowered the light in Macho's right hand until the beam rested on his watch, then on his air supply gauge. They had done this regularly throughout the dive.

Pointing his thumb back the way they had come, Josh thought, *Our bottom time shows we'd better turn around. The air supply says the same.*

Using his right hand, Macho touched the gloved fingers to his thumb, signaling "Okay." Then he turned around, Josh following.

Macho flashed the light back the way the boys had come. Josh, a little behind, saw his companion's sudden hand signal, "Stop!" Macho turned his hand down and quickly swung it back and forth, indicating, "Something's wrong!"

Josh saw it then, and his heart almost stopped. The light showed the water through which they had swum—and through which they now had to swim back—was no longer crystal clear. In fact, it was completely filled with tiny particles that made it impossible to see more than a few inches ahead!

Macho rapidly flipped the beam around to show that it could not penetrate the cloudy water.

What happened? Josh's mind screamed as he fought sudden panic. *Oh, of course! Our fins stirred up the sulfur when we passed through! Visibility's down to about eight inches! And the light's reflecting back from that gunk, so it's even harder to see!*

The murky water had imprisoned the boys deep inside the sunken submarine. A sharp, overpowering fear engulfed Josh. His heart leaped into a terrified pace. There was no safety line to follow back to the one open hatch, and the only way out was through the silent, deadly curtain of silted water.

It would take much more time now to find their way through the sub—if they could discover the way out at all. That would use up their precious air. *We could die here!* Josh's mind warned. *And it's my own fault!*

He was startled to feel Macho's hand suddenly grab his and tug. Josh moved his fins, driving his face close to the other boy's. Through the mask, Josh could see Macho's eyes were open wide in fright. Macho's abrupt, irregular hand movements, flashing the light at the terrifying sight before them, also made Josh aware that Macho was about to panic.

Can't let that happen! Josh thought, taking a firm grip on his own terror. Realizing that losing their heads would certainly cost their lives, he fought back a terrible urge to swim frantically, blindly, into the thick mass of floating cloud.

Got to stay together, Josh warned himself. *If we get separated, it'll all be over for the one without a light. I'd better take it and hang on to Macho.*

Josh swallowed hard and took Macho's free hand. Neither boy would have thought of holding hands under normal circumstances, but here it was a matter of life and death. Then Josh gently started removing the light from Macho's other hand. He resisted, then slowly released his grip.

Josh took the light in his right hand, thinking, *It looks as if the batteries are getting weak.* The thought scared him again. *Maybe it's just that the beam can't penetrate that stuff very well,* he told himself.

Guessing at what he hoped was the middle point between deck, bulkheads* and ceiling, Josh pointed the light ahead. *Got to keep my head!* he cautioned himself. *Macho's already on the edge of panic. If he sees me acting scared, he'll lose control and we'll both die!*

Slowly, carefully, holding Macho's right hand with his left, Josh began swimming through the terrifying wall of cloudy water. Macho moved beside him.

Josh tried to not think about all the mistakes he'd made that had brought him to this potential tragedy. He forced his mind to concentrate on finding a way out before it was too late. *Try to remember each room we passed through—*

His thought was snapped off as something in the murky gloom snagged his air hose, almost snatching the mouthpiece from his clenched teeth. Josh knew instantly that he had hooked onto one of the countless hanging pipes he'd seen on the swim in. Carefully, trying not to disturb the water any more than necessary, Josh brought the light around close. Through the cloud, he saw the problem and eased the hose free.

With a silent prayer of thanks, Josh again glanced at his instruments. *Watch, depth gauge, compass and air supply. Time's running out. Air's getting low. Light's getting weaker. Stop it! Don't think of the problems—think of how to get out safely!*

I'm so scared! he thought. *Oh, Lord! I've never been so scared!*

Josh's heart pounded so loudly he thought he could hear it against his eardrums. He fought a desire to breathe faster, knowing that would use up his precious air supply more rapidly. He kept swallowing, trying to dislodge the chunk of fear stuck in his throat. And in his mind he resolved, *If we get out of here alive—I mean* when *we get out of here—I'm never again going to let anybody make me do something I don't want to do! Never! Never!*

Macho gripped Josh's left hand so tightly it ached. Josh barely noticed, but he was aware that the other boy had changed. His brash self-assuredness was gone. He was like a little child, frightened and uncertain, trusting another person to lead the way.

Josh willed his speeding heart to slow, knowing that fear drove the beat up. As he pushed the weakening light through the silent, murky water, he followed each precious half-foot of visibility, his fins moving slowly when he wanted to kick wildly.

There's no use looking at my watch again, he told himself. *We're going as fast as we can. If I see how fast the time's passing, I might really panic!*

When he judged they'd swum a hundred feet, Josh stopped and signaled Macho to do the same. Slowly, Josh swung the light around the compartment. It was the largest they had explored. *This is where we entered the sub!* Josh thought with a surge of hope. *But either that light's getting weak fast or this compartment's got even less visibility than the others!*

Though it scared him to know for sure, he lowered the light to check his watch and air supply once more. He gulped. *Only a few minutes left! Got to find that hatch fast! But where is it?*

Still holding Macho's hand, Josh swam slowly upward, then stopped, treading water. *Can't see a thing! We're wasting time!* he thought. *We've got to have enough air left to make the ascent slowly or we'll get the bends. There's got to be a way to find that open hatch without having to feel every inch of this compartment!*

Josh closed his eyes and tried to envision the hatch somewhere overhead. Slowly, fighting the terror that wanted to seize him, he forced himself to see the compartment as it was when the boys entered.

That hatch is right about—there, Josh thought, looking upward and pointing the light. Its weak beam almost mocked his efforts to see. He could now see only three or four inches ahead. But in his mind's eye, he envisioned the open hatch through the murky water.

Squeezing Macho's hand, Josh began moving his fins upward through the silent cloud. He played the light about, seeking desperately for confirmation of the hatch's location. His light seemed to dim noticeably by the second.

Not much left of these batteries, he reminded himself. *Both time and air are running out fast! Unless we find that hatch soon—*

Suddenly he stopped swimming and squeezed Macho's hand hard. With the light, Josh pointed upward. "There!" Josh said the word aloud, causing an explosion of bubbles from his regulator.

About four feet away, a pale blue patch of light showed overhead. *The hatchway!* Josh's mind screamed in silent joy. *We've found it!*

Still gripping hands, both boys swam eagerly upward through the last of the murky water. The light gave out just as they eased through the hatch and into the open sea.

Josh released Macho's hand, and the boys headed for the surface—and a terrible surprise.

Chapter Ten

A SURPRISE AT THE SURFACE

J osh kept his eager face tilted toward the natural light as he and Macho started for the ocean's surface far above. *Not too fast!* Josh reminded himself. *That'll cause the bends!* Yet he had to fight a powerful urge to break through the water's last restraining hold. *Air's low because we've been down longer than we expected, but we'll make it! Don't panic now!*

Macho's long ordeal in the sub had robbed him of his usual bravado. He kept trying to rise too fast, forcing Josh to reach out and hold him back. Each time Josh did that, Macho's eyes were wide behind his mask.

In agonizingly slow stages, the boys moved upward a few feet at a time, stopping often so any deadly bubbles in their bloodstreams could dissolve. *Hope our air lasts,* Josh told himself, stealing a fearful glance at the fast-dropping gauge.

He wondered which would be worse: getting the bends or running out of air. *Stop it!* he told himself fiercely. Then he tried to think of soothing things—psalms, a prayer he'd learned as a little boy, safety coming closer.

In the seemingly forever rise toward the surface, Josh made some firm decisions. *I'm not going to let Macho make me do things I know are wrong! Not even if he does tell my secret! I'd have a better chance with Soviet spies than with letting him force me into dumb things like this!*

Josh also made a silent promise to himself on something else. *I'm going to make up with Tank,* he thought. *I'll also explain everything to Dad and Mom. Some secrets shouldn't be kept from parents, no matter what kind of promise is involved! Besides, I ought to be able to trust them more than a new friend like Macho.*

The boys finished their last stop in trying to avoid the bends. Safety was just a few feet away now. *As soon as we get back to shore,* Josh promised himself, *I'm going to tell Macho! He likes to boast that he's his own man. Well, from now on, I'm my own person again, and he's not going to make me change!*

Belatedly, Josh formed a wordless prayer of thanks just as his head broke through the surface beside the boat.

"Whooee!" Josh yelled, yanking off his regulator and throwing his other hand joyfully into the bright sunshine. "We made it! We made it!"

Macho surfaced at the same instant, but his reaction was different. Instead of shouting with relief, he removed his regulator and peered down at the silent, black shape 135 feet below. His face was white, and his eyes were still wide with fright.

"You okay?" Josh asked anxiously.

Wordlessly, Macho nodded, still looking down at the steel hulk that had almost been their tomb.

"Then let's get aboard!" Josh said, turning toward the power craft bouncing on the small waves beside him. He removed his scuba gear and started to hand it up to the men who had brought the boys to the dive site, but he suddenly stopped, his arm suspended in midair. "Hey! This isn't our boat!" he cried. "This is a Boston Whaler!"

Nancy Hogan and Jack Simms leaned over the side of the boat. "Jack and I borrowed this," Nancy said softly. "We sent the two men ashore who brought you boys out here. We waited because we have a message for you."

Alarm shot through Josh. "Message?" he repeated. "What message?" His eyes flicked from Nancy's face to Jack's. Both appeared grave with concern.

"Get in and we'll tell you on the way to shore."

Josh's heart thumped in apprehension as he and Macho climbed into the boat and removed their equipment. Macho was still strangely silent. He sat stiffly in a seat, eyes fixed and staring into space. Jack took the controls and turned the whaler toward shore.

"Tell me!" Josh urged, looking across at Nancy and already imagining all kinds of terrible things.

"Josh," Nancy began, "I'm sorry to be the one to tell you, but—"

"Tell me what? What's happened?"

"Josh, your father's been in an accident. Your mother

sent us—"

"Accident?" Josh interrupted, his voice shooting up in fear. "What kind of accident?"

"A car crash, that's all I know. Jack and I were getting out of the elevator when your mother came running out of your condo screaming. She said something about just getting a phone call and having to go to the hospital in Wailuku.* Her husband had been hurt in an accident. She was so upset it was hard to understand."

Josh moaned and shook his head. "Dad's hurt? How bad?"

"I'm sorry," Nancy answered, reaching out to touch the boy's arm gently. "Your mother didn't say. But we told her we'd get you and take you to her at the hospital right away. We had to wait for you boys to surface...."

Josh didn't hear the rest. His mind reeled under the unexpected news. He glanced at Macho, who didn't seem to have been listening. He still stared at the sea where they'd dived on the *Bluegill*. Josh thought Macho was in shock and not really seeing anything.

Turning back to Nancy, Josh bombarded her with questions. She was sympathetic but insisted she didn't know anything more.

The moment the Boston Whaler touched shore, Jack jumped out and helped Nancy and the boys. "My car's right over there," he said, pointing. "I'll bring your equipment. You get in and we'll be on our way to the hospital."

Josh helped Macho into the back seat and buckled both

their seat belts. Jack took the wheel, with Nancy beside him. Doors slammed, and the car pulled out onto the highway and headed south. Maalaea Bay* was that way. Josh knew that near there the car would turn north toward the twin cities of Wailuku and Kahului* on the other side of the island. The hospital was there.

Lord, Josh prayed silently, *take care of my dad, please!* Then he leaned forward and asked, "Jack, can't we go any faster?"

"I'm going as fast as the law allows! We don't want the police stopping us for speeding, do we? That'd only delay us."

"Jack's going as fast as he safely can," Nancy added soothingly. "Sit back and try to relax. There's nothing you can do until we get there."

Josh glanced to see if there were any white patrol cars with their blue lights around. Hawaii has no state highway patrol. Police enforce road safety in and out of the towns, and their cars have only blue lights.

What could have happened to Dad? Josh wondered as the car swept along the narrow, rural road. It threaded its way between the ocean on the right and the canefields and West Maui Mountains on the left.

Josh turned to look at Macho, whose appearance was getting better. His eyes were no longer open and staring. Color was slowly returning to his face.

"Macho," Josh asked quietly, "you okay?"

"I guess so. I keep thinking of being down there in that

sub. When I get to a phone—"

Phone! The word exploded in Josh's brain. He sat stiffly upright, a wild thought possessing him. *Nancy said Mom got a phone call about Dad, but there's no phone in our condo! And my parents didn't know where I was going this morning! So how did Nancy and Jack know where to find Macho and me?*

Josh looked sharply at Jack Simms behind the wheel. The man's face showed no emotion. Nancy's face was likewise a mask. *I don't understand why—yes!* Josh thought. *The Soviet sub!*

The truth hit Josh so hard he flinched, fear seizing him. To confirm it, he leaned closer to Macho and whispered, "Macho, did you tell either Nancy or Jack about you know what?"

Macho frowned, seeming to have trouble concentrating. Then he shook his head. "Why would I do that? It's a secret," he whispered.

Josh shot a quick glance at the two adults in the front seat. They didn't seem concerned about the boys' heads being so close together. Josh almost hissed, "Macho, are you *sure* you didn't tell either of them?"

Macho hesitated, then shrugged as he said, "Well, Nancy's such a nice woman, so I didn't figure it'd hurt to—"

"I knew it!" Josh's whisper almost got away from him. "I knew it!"

"You knew what?"

"A second ago, I just thought of something! My parents

didn't know where I was going this morning!"

The other boy frowned, slow to understand. "They didn't?"

"No, and neither did yours, did they?"

Macho shook his head.

"Then the only way Nancy and Jack could have known where we were was to have followed us!"

"But why would they do that?"

"Because my dad hasn't been in an accident, and we're not being taken to the hospital! They're not driving carefully to avoid a speeding ticket! They just don't want to attract the police!"

Macho was suddenly alert but still confused. "I don't get it," he said.

"Don't you see?" Josh said softly but with conviction. "Nancy and Jack are Soviet agents!"

Macho jerked as though Josh had slapped him.

"And," Josh added in a terse whisper, "they've taken us prisoners!"

Chapter Eleven

PRISONERS!

Half an hour later, Josh and Macho were seated side by side in a darkened room. They weren't tied, yet escape wasn't possible. Their jail was an abandoned house at the end of a long, dirt road. Nancy Hogan guarded the only door. Cardboard had been nailed over the two windows, making the room gloomy.

Jack Simms bent over the boys, a blackjack* sticking up out of his hip pocket. "I'm getting tired of waiting!" he said with barely controlled fury. "You'd better tell us where our sub is!"

Macho cringed in what remained of an old rattan chair. "I already told you, I don't know!" he cried. Jabbing a quivering forefinger at Josh, he continued, "Only he knows!"

"Well?" Jack said, turning to Josh.

Josh sat on an empty packing crate, his trembling hands gripping the splintery sides. He gulped, trying to swallow the lump of fear that had been threatening to choke him since the agents had confirmed the kidnapping in the car.

112

Nancy had already explained she first became suspicious when she found Josh's photocopied newspaper clipping in her car. She figured the boys' interest in the sub was more than they'd let on. Then she learned Josh's secret from Macho.

"I—I can't tell you!" Josh said, looking at Jack.

"You'll tell me, one way or another!"

"Jack, please!" Nancy said. She tugged on his arm until he straightened up, then eased herself between him and the boy. "Let me try again."

"You already wasted valuable time and got nowhere!" Jack reminded her, his voice hard but not loud. "Let me do it my way and these kids'll tell us—fast!"

"We won't have to hurt them if they cooperate. Now please go check outside," she urged, gently pushing Jack toward the door. "Make sure nobody's around."

"You know nobody's ever going to find this place, Nancy! Just give me five minutes alone with—"

"Please, Jack! Outside!"

Josh licked his dry lips as the grumbling man walked through the door. The late afternoon sun streamed in from just above the horizon. Darkness would come soon. Josh glimpsed a sparkling piece of the ocean through huge old kiawe* trees and heard waves hitting the shore before the door slammed. The room was in semidarkness again.

"Now," the woman said quietly, "I kept Jack from tying you both up like a sack of potatoes. I've kept him from hurting you—so far. But he's not a patient man, and I'm not sure how long it'll be before he does something drastic—unless you answer our questions."

"I already told you a thousand times!" Macho said in a hoarse whisper. "I just saw the tape! I don't know where it is now! And I don't know where the sub sank!"

Josh was still getting over the pain of having Macho break his word. Macho obviously hadn't listened to his own warnings about the danger of betraying that confidence.

"How about it, Josh?" Nancy asked, kneeling to look him squarely in the eyes. "You don't want to see your friend hurt, do you?"

Josh only shook his head.

"Good! Then you tell us now, and you'll both be home in time for dinner."

Josh took a slow, deep breath, trying to think, to stall for time. In a voice that threatened to crack he asked, "Could Macho and I talk this over—alone?"

Nancy considered the request, then rose, nodding. "I'll give you just five minutes." She turned to Macho and added, "You'd better convince him before Jack comes back."

The last rays of sunlight from the sinking sun beamed briefly as the woman opened the door. Josh again heard waves crashing against the shore. Then the door closed, and the boys were alone.

"Tell them, Josh!" Macho leaped up from his chair and waved his arms wildly. "Tell them before it's too late!"

Josh got up and hurried to the nearest window, where

he pulled one edge of the cardboard loose. Through the dirty window pane, he saw that stout plywood had been nailed across the outside. "No way out there," he said quietly, shaking his head.

He quickly crossed the room to the only other window and found the same barriers. Turning to Macho, he said with forced quietness, "We'll have to find some other escape if we want to get out of this in one piece."

Grabbing Josh's shoulder roughly, Macho demanded, "What's that mean?"

"Think about it. This isn't some game, Macho! This is international intrigue! Real spies! They can't let us go, not even if I give them the tape and tell them exactly where that sub sank."

Macho dropped his voice to a surprised whisper as he asked, "Are you saying that no matter what we do, they're never going to let us go?"

Josh nodded and finished his inspection of the room. It was bare except for the rude furniture on which the boys had been seated, a broken-down table with three legs, and a few empty cardboard boxes.

"They can't, Macho," he said. "They can't risk having us tell who they are. And time's running out for them, too, so they're really desperate. Our navy's sitting all around their sub. They can't recover it now. The best they can hope for is that we'll give them the location so they can sneak in there underwater and blow it up before our guys recover its secrets. So we've got to give our navy the time it needs to help protect our country!"

"We'd promise not to tell!" Macho's voice was a frightened whimper. "We'd say we never—"

"Stop it!" Josh commanded, grabbing Macho by both shoulders. "Face the facts! You can see what they're doing! Jack is trying to scare us into telling. Nancy is pretending to be nice, but they both want the same thing! If we—I—tell, then they don't need us anymore!"

Macho opened his mouth to protest, then closed it with a snap of teeth. He pulled away from Josh's grip and collapsed weakly in his chair. "You're probably right!" he moaned. "They can't let us go, no matter what! But— what do you think they'll do to us?"

Josh was scared, but he had just lived through a near tragedy on the *Bluegill* that had seemed pretty hopeless at the time, too, and God had delivered him. So he said a silent prayer and tried to encourage Macho. "Let's not think about that," he said. "Instead, let's try to think how to stall them."

"Stall?" Macho straightened up hopefully. "How will we do that?"

"I'm not sure, but we're not tied by ropes or anything, so maybe we'll get a chance to escape."

"Jack's a lot stronger than us, and besides, he's got that blackjack!"

"I know, but at least we're on land. Maui* is a small island. My parents will have the authorities searching for us, and if they find the two divers who took us to the

Bluegill, they'll describe Jack and Nancy. That'll give the police something to go on."

"But how'll they find us at this place? You saw when we drove in—it's back so far off the main road that not even surfers or divers have used this trail! Those old trees probably hide the shack from the air—"

"Stop looking at the dark side!" Josh snapped. "But you've got a point. If we can't get away, we need some way of bringing the authorities to us."

"Fat chance of that! There's no phone, no radio—nothing in this old shack!"

"We've got to find a way, Macho! But that means we've got to stall! Get time to think—"

He broke off as an engine started up outside.

"What's that?" Macho asked, cocking his ear to listen. "Sounds like a motorboat."

"I think it is. Probably—" Josh cut himself short.

"Probably what?"

"Nothing." Josh didn't want to finish his thought.

Macho's eyes opened wide in understanding. "I know what you're thinking! They're probably going to take us out in the ocean and—"

"Cut that out!" Josh interrupted. "Save your energy for thinking! We've got to get out of this mess!"

"How can you be so calm?" Macho cried. "Every second is bringing us closer to—"

"I'm not calm! Inside, my heart's trying to jump through my chest, and my tongue's so dry I can hardly talk. But I'm trying to think—"

The door opened abruptly. Nancy walked in first, leaving the door ajar. Jack followed a step behind, thumping the blackjack in the palm of his left hand and also leaving the door open. The sun had almost disappeared. Josh heard the motorboat idling in the water.

"Well?" the man demanded, advancing menacingly toward the boys. "What's your decision?"

Josh started to shake his head, but Macho leaped up and cried, "I don't know anything except what I told you! Please let me go! Josh's the only one you want! Please! Please!"

This further betrayal hit Josh like a knife in the back, but he wasn't surprised. Macho had broken his word and told Josh's secret, putting both their lives in jeopardy and possibly Josh's family, too. In the submarine, Josh had thought maybe Macho was changing, but apparently not. He was concerned only about saving his own skin.

Jack's lip curled in scorn. "You little coward!" he growled at Macho. "You're disgusting!"

"Stop wasting time, Jack!" Nancy ordered, touching his arm lightly. Turning to Josh, she said, "One last chance."

Josh tried to think of something brave to say, but his mind was on his objective: stall and think. "Could I have a little more time?" he asked.

"No more time!" Jack snapped.

"No!" Macho screeched, jumping up. "Tell them, Josh! Tell them!" He looked around wildly, then at the open door. Instantly, he darted toward it, crouching to slip between Jack and Nancy.

Jack's hand shot out hard and fast. He grabbed Macho by the wrist and used his own momentum to swing him around. Macho sprawled to the bare wood floor and lay there whimpering from a tightly curled position. All his bravado was gone.

Josh tried again. "If I could have just a little more time—"

"Quit stalling!" Jack commanded. He grabbed Josh's right wrist and bent over Macho, then yanked him to his feet. "Into the boat with you two!"

The boys were half-carried, half-dragged toward a small fishing boat with inboard engine and a cabin. The craft idled at a short dock sticking out into a small bay.

Josh looked around quickly, hoping to see some way out. There was nothing except a few puffy clouds overhead. They turned glorious shades of pink from the sun now set beyond the ocean's horizon.

Jack deposited the boys inside the cabin on a U-shaped bench that ran around the wheel and control console. "What're you going to do with us?" Macho asked fearfully.

Jack ignored the question and turned to Nancy. "Bring their gear in here," he instructed.

"Our gear?" Macho cried. "But we're about out of air from diving on the *Bluegill*! We can't make another—"

"I know," Jack said with a grim smile. "We've already

checked your gauges."

Macho started to say something as full understanding swept over him. His mouth worked, but no words came.

While Nancy and Jack cast off the safety lines holding the boat to the dock, Josh looked around frantically. *There's got to be something we can do!* he thought. His eyes desperately surveyed the cabin. *Nothing! Noth—wait!*

Josh's gaze fell on an orange-colored cylinder clipped to the side of the control console. Looking closer, he saw that the unfamiliar gadget was about a foot long, four inches across, with a small wire protruding from one end. He had never seen anything like it, but his heart jumped. *I just remembered something the Coast Guard officer said!* he thought. *That must be an emergency radio beacon!*

How did it work? Josh tried to recall. *Either by being turned upside down, like when a boat capsizes, or by flipping a switch.*

In his eagerness, Josh pushed himself to his feet, his eyes scanning the orange-colored cylinder.

"Sit down, kid!" Jack ordered, leaping up from forcing Macho into his scuba gear. Josh was shoved back so hard that he crashed against the console. Slowly, he slid to the cabin deck.

Josh lay there, half-stunned, the orange cylinder between his right arm and ribs. With speeding heart, he watched the man and woman make final preparations for getting under way. Slowly, carefully, Josh turned his body to the left so that Nancy and Jack couldn't see what he was doing with his right hand. His fingers eased along the cool, metal tube. *Got to find the switch!* Josh thought despairingly. *There!*

Just as he started to flip it, Jack turned around. "Okay," he said, "Macho's ready. Now it's your turn, Josh. You'd better talk!"

The boy felt panic sweep over him. His right forefinger was on the switch, but if Jack saw him....

"Get up!" Jack ordered.

Josh lay still, desperately thinking how to turn on the switch without being seen.

"I said, 'Get up!' " Jack repeated. He reached down and yanked the boy by his left arm. "Now!"

Josh's hidden forefinger and thumb closed on the toggle switch. As he was jerked violently to his feet, he snapped on the switch.

Chapter Twelve

DESPERATE MOMENTS

The two boys, in full scuba gear, were forced onto the deck and made to sit with their backs against the wall of the small cabin. Nancy watched them from the stern while Jack went to the controls. The engine revved up, and the fishing boat headed out to sea.

A thousand thoughts filled Josh's mind. *Was that round, orange thing what I think it was? Did I really turn it on? Is it working? Does it make a sound that Jack might hear above the engine? Is anybody receiving the signal if it is working? If it is, sooner or later, they'll come investigate! So we've got to stall for time!*

Josh glanced over at Macho. *He looks so pitiful! I'd like to give him some hope, but I can't trust him anymore. What's going to happen now?*

Night soon hid the boat except for the red and green running lights. The moon hadn't yet risen, though thousands of stars blazed overhead. Inland, Josh glimpsed lights, but he saw nothing that could help him or Macho out of their desperate situation.

"Please! Can't you tell them?" Macho whispered. "Maybe they'll let us go!"

"No, they won't. And I can't tell, because it's not just our safety at stake. Our country's security is also involved. Can't you see that?"

Macho sighed slowly, and Josh could feel him shudder in the darkness. Then Macho asked quietly, "When're they going to—" His voice broke, and he couldn't finish the sentence.

Josh didn't answer immediately. His thoughts raced around in confused circles. Yet, slowly, his mind cleared. He decided to offer encouragement. "They're just trying to scare us," he said.

"They're doing a good job of that!"

Josh almost smiled. "Have you noticed we're not that far from shore yet and they're running back and forth?"

"What for?"

"Maybe they're trying to look like a real fishing boat that's pulling a net. That's less likely to attract attention than heading straight out to sea at top speed."

"Nobody'll see us! There hasn't been another boat anywhere on the water since we started almost an hour ago!"

"I don't think they're really going to hurt us! Remember, we're the only ones who know where their sub is."

"You mean *you're* the only one! They don't need me!"

"Maybe they're afraid to do anything to you because

then I'd know for sure the same thing was going to happen to me. That'd make me less willing to tell them what they want to know."

With that, the boys fell silent for a time, listening to the throb of the engine and watching the shore lights disappear. As the lights dimmed, so did their hopes.

An hour later, knowing they were now well out to sea, Josh was trying to think of how to stall for time when he realized, *Uh-oh! Jack's cut the engine!* Nancy turned around at the stern, where she had been looking out over the darkened water. Jack started out from the cabin.

Josh whispered to Macho, "I've got an idea how to stall for more time! Just don't say anything! I'm going to try something."

Just then Jack reached down and pulled both boys to their feet. "Time for your dive, boys," he said with a grin.

Josh desperately looked across the black ocean. No ships appeared; no lights approached. He turned his head as the man adjusted both boys' air tanks on their backs.

"We'll never be able to swim back to shore from here," Josh said.

"I gave you your chance," Jack replied evenly, pulling both boys by the wrist toward the stern.

Nancy unsnapped the two chains that acted as extensions of the rail across the stern opening. "Yes," she said into the darkness, "you don't leave us with any other choice."

Josh gulped as he repeated to himself, *I'm the only lead*

they have! They don't dare hurt me! But then he thought, *What if I'm wrong? What if they're not just trying to scare me into talking?*

"Do something!" Macho hissed.

Josh felt Jack's hand forcing him over the stern. The boy whispered, "Lord, I need wisdom! Please?" Aloud he cried, "Wait!"

The hand on his back stopped shoving. "Why should we?" Jack growled.

Josh thought of the orange cylinder in the cabin. *Is it working?* he wondered. *Maybe somebody's already checking it out! Got to stall.*

"Well?" Nancy asked.

"Uh, if I tell you," Josh said, his stomach rising and falling like the boat, "will you let us go?"

"Absolutely!" Nancy said.

"The minute we have what we want," Jack added.

"Well, then, do you have some paper and a pencil? I could draw a map and put in the compass points as best as I remember them."

A couple of minutes later, Josh was leaning against the console inside the cabin with pen and paper. He and Macho still had on their complete scuba gear, including fins. Nancy and Jack were standing close behind, trying to look over his shoulder.

Josh tried not to look at the orange gadget. *Is it making a sound?* he wondered. Aloud he said, "I can't think with you two standing over me like that! Go out on deck and leave us alone!"

"No tricks," Jack warned. "You can't get away."

"Jack!" Nancy suddenly cut in urgently. "Look!"

Josh turned to follow the woman's pointing finger. Through the cabin window, he saw the running lights of a large vessel farther out to sea. The single white light at the top of the mast showed it was a much bigger craft than the fishing boat.

Coast Guard! Josh wanted to yell, but he kept quiet, his heart pounding.

The two agents hurried onto the deck, leaving Josh and Macho standing inside the cabin.

"Even if it's a ship, they won't help us," Macho said mournfully. "They don't know we're in trouble!"

Josh glanced again at the orange cylinder. *Maybe they do,* he told himself. To Macho he said, "Macho, are you willing to do anything to save our lives?"

"That's a dumb question!"

"Then listen! If we can slip over the side and into the water, maybe we can hide in the darkness."

"We can't make it back to shore, so why bother? And anyway, how can we hide when we can't dive? Have you forgotten our tanks are almost out of air?"

"We could dive if we had to and hope there's enough air to get us by until we can surface again."

"They'll turn on lights and find us on top of the water!"

"You got any other ideas? Besides, help *may* be on its way."

Macho sighed and shook his head, disbelieving but having no alternative plan to offer.

"Then let's do it! If they just keep watching that big boat—"

Josh didn't finish his sentence, because just then Jack and Nancy reentered the cabin. "It passed by," she said. "Let's see what you've drawn for us, Josh."

The boy's heart jumped as he thought of the blank sheet of paper. As the man and woman approached, Macho suddenly stiffened. "Helicopter!" he said, cocking his head. "Hear it?"

All four people turned to peer out the cabin window.

"It's a chopper, all right!" Nancy exclaimed. "Flashing a searchlight around the water! Quick, cut those running lights!"

Jack leaped to the console and rapidly hit switches, plunging the cabin into total darkness. Outside, both the red and green running lights were also dark. But Josh saw a silvery sheen on the water. *The moon!* he thought. *It's risen! Maybe the chopper can see us even without our lights on!*

The two spies picked their way through the darkened cabin to stand close to the window. The searchlight from the sky continued to sweep the ocean's surface in the distance.

"Must be the Coast Guard searching for somebody," Jack muttered. "Maybe some fisherman was reported overdue."

"At least they're searching in the other direction," Nancy said. "For now."

Josh leaned close to Macho's ear and whispered, "If they go outside to look closer, let's slip out the side door and into the water!"

From the window, Nancy said, "If they hit us with that light and see we don't have running lights on, they'll get suspicious and come investigate!"

"They're still heading away—no! They're turning this way!" Jack exclaimed.

"Flying a search pattern," Nancy said. "I'm going outside to see better."

"Me, too."

As soon as the spies had gone onto the stern deck, Josh whispered, "Let's go!"

Walking quietly in scuba gear and flippers was difficult, but the boys eased out the side door and over to the nearest rail. There Josh swung one leg over and straddled it in preparation for diving.

"I'm scared!" Macho whispered.

"Me, too! But we've got no choice. Ready?"

"They'll hear us when we land in the water!"

Josh pulled his swim mask into place and hissed, "Got your regulator ready?"

"Yes, but that'll use up what little air—"

"Hey!" Jack's startled voice cut through the moonlit night. "What're you kids doing?"

"Dive!" Josh yelled just before he shoved his regulator

into place and leaped clear of the boat.

As he hit the water, the moonlight was bright enough that he saw Macho land beside him. Both boys allowed themselves to sink well below the surface.

I sure hope they can't find us, Josh thought, *and that the Coast Guard finds them before we run out of air!*

Josh and Macho swam side by side underwater, Josh guiding them away from the boat. A small, white light danced across the surface. *Flashlight,* Josh thought. *Nancy and Jack are trying to find us. They know we don't have much air and will have to surface soon! Oh, Lord, don't let them find us before the chopper—*

Josh's thought was broken off as Macho suddenly gripped his arm hard and shook it. He turned to see through his bubbles, and his first thought was *Shark!* But he sensed that wasn't what had made Macho grab his arm so tightly. The moon wasn't much help at that depth, but Josh could just make out Macho's right hand in front of his chest. The hand moved back and forth, left to right, signaling "I'm out of air!"

It was one of the hardest things he had ever done, but Josh removed his mouthpiece with his right hand. With his left, he motioned to his mouth, signaling "Buddy breathing system. I'll share my air with you."

Macho grabbed the regulator. Josh wanted to shout, "Easy! That's all we've got left!" but there was no way to warn his companion.

Instead, Josh used his circled thumb and forefinger to

signal "Okay!" He had an anxious moment as Macho kept the regulator when he reached to take it back, making him wonder if Macho were going to keep the air all to himself. Finally, however, Macho handed the regulator back to Josh, and he sighed inwardly with relief.

Though Josh couldn't see his gauge in the dark water, he knew he was almost out of air, too. He gripped Macho's arm and pointed upward.

Macho seemed to understand, and the boys angled toward the surface just as Josh realized, *I'm out of oxygen!* Then he wondered, *Are we far enough from the boat to be safe, or will they see us and grab us again?* He hated to think what might happen if they were captured a second time.

They broke the surface together as quietly as possible. The flashlight was working across the water to their right. After a couple of quick breaths of fresh air, Josh whispered, "Drop everything except your fins and mask!"

They had done so and were starting to swim with their hands and feet underwater so they wouldn't make any noise when a small light hit them. From the nearby fishing boat's deck, Nancy exclaimed, "There they are!"

"Swim fast!" Josh cried in the moonlight. "If they catch us again...."

The roar of the engine's starting drowned out his final words. The boys swam frantically as the darkened boat bore down on them.

"They're trying to run us over!" Macho shouted.

"They're not going to stop!"

Josh shuddered, thinking what the boat's propeller could do to them. "Dive!" he yelled, taking a deep breath. He brought his feet up high, cleared the surface, and started to force his head down in a fast tuck dive.

As his face entered the water, Josh glimpsed a big searchlight from the sky striking the fishing boat. Underwater, Josh heard the churning of the boat's propeller. *We're not deep enough!* his mind screamed as he used all his strength to stroke down.

Suddenly, the engine sound changed sharply. *They're turning away!* Josh realized. *But why?*

He was already feeling the need for another breath of air when he got his answer. He heard a second, bigger boat engine in the distance, moving fast. *Coast Guard!* he thought.

Josh couldn't go deeper—not with the growing need to breathe. He didn't want to risk being struck by the heavier screws of the much larger boat approaching at full speed, but he had to surface fast.

Macho was nowhere in sight as Josh drove his fins hard toward the life-giving oxygen at the surface. He exploded from the water and gulped air. Then, turning toward the oncoming vessel, he threw his arms high into the sky, waved them wildly, and shouted, "We're here! Don't run us down!"

Josh thought he heard an echo, but then he realized Macho was yelling and waving his arms a few feet away.

A moment later, he also realized the larger craft was turning away, following the fishing boat. But in the moonlight, he saw the distinctive, bright-orange stripe on the big cutter's white side. "Coast Guard, Macho!" he yelled. "Look!"

As the chase continued with the larger craft rapidly overtaking the smaller, Josh saw something fall between them and the moon to land with a plop a few feet away. The helicopter's big searchlight showed clearly what it was.

"Life raft!" Josh shouted. "Macho, we've been saved!"

Chapter Thirteen

LESSONS LEARNED

Three days later, Josh stood on the lanai* of the rented condo with his father. Over a forty-eight-hour period, Josh had been questioned secretly in a secluded part of Honolulu by the same man who had interrogated his father earlier.

Now the boy was back in the family's rented condo, where it was peaceful and quiet. He gazed through binoculars across Maalaea Bay.* Beyond Molokini* and Kahoolawe,* he could see two strange ships on the horizon. One had something like oil derricks rising from the deck. The other was long and flat, like a barge.

"Just like the pictures in the Honolulu papers when they raised that Soviet sub in 1968, huh, Dad?"

His father took the glasses and studied the horizon, then said, "I guess they're about ready to try raising the robot sub."

Josh watched the naval ships patrolling around the salvage vessels. "But we'll probably never know for sure if the robot is recovered or not," he added. "The authorities won't tell us any more this time than they did before."

Mr. Ladd lowered the binoculars and said, "One thing's for sure, Son. The Soviets never got to the sub you saw sink."

Josh nodded, feeling good inside.

"As the authorities said when they finished questioning you, 'Although you should have told your parents and us about the sub immediately, you were still very brave and helped keep our country safe.' "

"But they also said I must never tell anyone else about it," Josh said softly, "not even Tank or Tiffany or Nathan."

"That's the only way they can guarantee that you—and all of us—will be safe from other foreign agents. Otherwise, some might think the sub is still there for the taking and try to do what the first two failed to do. Only your mother and I know—plus you and Macho.

"Son," he added, "let's be grateful your little brother found that tape behind the chest of drawers and showed it to your mother and me."

Josh nodded, knowing his parents had viewed the cassette, then in alarm took it to the authorities. It was obvious to them why Josh had disappeared.

The authorities hadn't been able to understand why Macho had also vanished, however, until they questioned Tank. He'd kept Josh's secret until he was convinced that revealing it could save Josh's life. The authorities then guessed Macho *hadn't* kept the secret, which was why both boys had been kidnapped.

"So if Nathan hadn't done that," John Ladd added softly, "you might not be here now." His voice had a slight tremor as he fought to control his emotions.

For a moment, Josh felt annoyed because his nosy little brother had again prowled through his things. But then he smiled and said, "Too bad Nathan can't be told he helped capture some real spies!"

"Nathan's excited about the part you *could* tell—your dive into the *Bluegill*, and now the Navy's decision to raise the boat, cut it up, and sink it way out in deep water. Seems your little brother was so intrigued by your adventure in that sub that *he* wanted to try it someday."

"I'm glad he'll never get the chance!"

"I've told you before, Son, but I've got to say it again. You were very smart to activate that switch on the boat's emergency signaling device."

"I just remembered what the Coast Guard officer had said about always investigating, even though people sometimes turn it on accidentally. So I thought they'd come to investigate if I could turn it on in Jack and Nancy's boat—and if that's what that gadget really was. The terrible part was not knowing for sure."

"Well, it worked fine, Son. The monitoring station in Honolulu passed on the information to the authorities who had your tape. Then they figured out what might have happened. It was only a matter of time until they found you."

"For a while," Josh said with a weak smile, "I didn't

think anybody was going to find us before it was too late."

His mother's key sounded in the front door lock. Father and son turned to greet her as she came in.

"I saw Tank and Macho talking downstairs," she said. "Tank knows something's going on because you and Macho disappeared and all the authorities came around. But he naturally doesn't know the whole story. He told me he's dying to hear the rest."

"Macho won't tell him?" Josh asked in surprise.

"Apparently not. Maybe this last experience made Macho realize he must keep some secrets."

"I'd sure like to tell Tank everything, but I know I really can't."

"He'll understand," Mrs. Ladd said, touching her older son's cheek. "Tank's that kind of friend."

"But," Mr. Ladd added quickly, "some things must *not* be kept secret from parents. Right, Son?"

Josh nodded and said, "Dad, Mom, I'm very sorry about lying to you and all the foolish things I did with Macho, like diving on the *Bluegill* when you'd told me not to. I know I've ignored and disobeyed God, too. So I deserve whatever discipline you give me."

His father pursed his lips thoughtfully. "That discipline will be fair but firm, as the case requires," he said.

His mother added, "It's true that bad company corrupts good morals, as it says in 1 Corinthians 15:33."

"If Tank's downstairs, now might be a good time to apologize and make up with him, Son," Mr. Ladd suggested.

"I was just thinking the same thing."

As Josh started down in the elevator, it stopped at the second floor. The door slid open, and Igor started to get on, but he stopped at the sight of Josh.

The boy reached out impulsively and shook the man's hand. "Come in! Come in!" he said. "I've been wanting to talk to you!"

"Da?" Igor said with a doubtful frown.

"Yes! I misjudged you. What'd you want to talk to me about a few days ago?"

The elevator door closed, and Igor shrugged. "I try to varn you. Doze people—Nancy and Jack—someding about dem I don't trust. But I don't see dem no more. Maybe dey gone avay?"

"For a long time," Josh said. "Thanks, Igor!"

"You can't tell Igor vat's going on?"

The boy shook his head. His imagination had created an enemy agent where there was a friend. Two very real agents had given him the scare of his life. But he couldn't say that.

"Sorry," Josh said softly. "But thanks, Igor!"

Igor grinned as the elevator door slid open at the ground floor. The man and boy started walking across the grassy area, past the fragrant plumeria* shrub, when a voice called out, "Hey, Josh!"

Macho waved from where he stood talking with Tank beyond the swimming pool at the bay's edge. Josh said good-bye to Igor and moved uncertainly toward the other two boys. He felt a little scared inside, wondering what he could say to make up with Tank.

As Josh drew near, Macho greeted him by saying, "I was just telling Tank that neither you nor I can say what happened a couple of days ago, but you're the bravest guy I ever met!"

"Thanks, Macho."

"Please call me Ted, not Macho."

A few minutes later, the changed Ted had gone, leaving Josh and Tank alone. An awkward silence seemed to build between them until Josh couldn't stand it any longer. "Look, Tank," he blurted suddenly, "I'm sorry! I was really, really wrong!"

A smile spread across his friend's face. "Forget it," Tank said. "We're friends again, as always."

Josh was so relieved he wanted to shout. Instead, he clapped his best friend soundly on the right shoulder. "How about if we go surfing? Nothing bad can happen doing that!"

Before Tank could reply, Nathan came running up from where he'd been sunning himself on a nearby lounge chair. "I heard that," he said, "and I'm not so sure! You two will always find trouble, even in surfing!"

Josh grinned at his little brother. "Well, maybe so," he said, "but Tank and I will handle it, won't we?"

"Sure," Tank said, "as long as we're friends again."

"We're friends again," Josh affirmed, smiling so hard his face hurt. "Friends forever!"

GLOSSARY

Chapter One

Be-still tree: A short, poisonous tree with dense, green foliage and bright yellow flowers that fold up at night.

Breakwater: An offshore structure, such as a wall, used to protect a harbor or beach from the force of waves.

Conning tower: A submarine's low observation tower. Includes the main point of entry into the sub.

Haleakala: (*hol-ee-ahk-uh-la*) A dormant volcanic mountain (10,023 feet) on east Maui, located in Haleakala National Park.

Ironwood tree: A leafless tree with long, drooping, green needles. Sometimes called an Australian pine, in Hawaii this tree is used as a windbreak. Ironwood is sometimes cut and shaped like high hedges.

Kahoolawe: (*kah-hoe-la-vee*) An island of 45 square miles located about 10 miles southwest of Maui.

Kanahena Point: (*kay-na-heh-na*) A point of land on the southern tip of Maui.

Maalaea: (*ma-ah-lay-ah*) A village on the west side of Maalaea Bay that's a fishing and tourist port.

Maalaea Bay: (*ma-ah-lay-ah*) The large, open expanse of water on Maui's south shore. The islet of Molokini and the island of Kahoolawe are clearly visible from its shore.

Maui: (*mau-ee*) Second largest of the main Hawaiian islands; 728 square miles in area.

Molokini: (*ma-low-kee-nee*) An islet that's really the tip of an ancient volcano rising from the ocean floor. The U.S. Coast Guard maintains an unmanned beacon light on this uninhabited speck of land.

Port: The left side of a boat or ship as you look forward.

Rattan: (*ra-tan*) Part of the long, tough stem of a rattan palm tree; used in making wickerwork (a type of weaving) furniture.

Starboard: (*star-bard*) The right side of a boat or ship as you look forward.

Stern: The rear end of a boat or ship.

Chapter Two

Ahi: (*ah-hee*) Pacific yellowtail tuna.

Lahaina: (*la-high-na*) A town of 6,100 on the northwest coast of Maui. Once the whaling capital of the mid-Pacific, it's now a center of tourism, shopping and pineapple and sugarcane farming.

Maalaea Bay: (*ma-ah-lay-ah*) The large, open expanse of water on Maui's south shore. The islet of Molokini and the island of Kahoolawe are clearly visible from its shore.

Olowalu Point: (*oh-low-wa-loo*) A point of land on the western tip of Maui.

Scuba: (*skoo-ba*) Stands for "self-contained underwater breathing apparatus." It's a way of diving with a portable breathing unit consisting of compressed air in tanks, hoses and a mouthpiece. This gear allows free-swimming divers to go deeper than almost anyone had dreamed possible a few years ago.

Sling gun: A device used for underwater fishing, it employs an elastic band to propel a dart tied to the front of the gun.

Snorkeling: Swimming at or just below the surface with the face underwater so as to observe what's below. The swimmer uses a face mask and a tube with a mouthpiece at one end and the other end extending above the surface for air.

Undercover: Acting in secret.

Chapter Three

Aloha shirt: (*ah-low-hah*) A loose-fitting man's Hawaiian shirt worn outside the pants. The garment is usually very colorful.

Lahaina: (*la-high-na*) A town of 6,100 on the northwest coast of Maui. Once the whaling capital of the mid-

Pacific, it's now a center of tourism, shopping and pineapple and sugarcane farming.

Lanai: (*la-nye*) A patio, porch or balcony. Also the name of a small Hawaiian island west of Maui.

Maalaea Bay: (*ma-ah-lay-ah*) The large, open expanse of water on Maui's south shore. The islet of Molokini and the island of Kahoolawe are clearly visible from its shore.

Maui: (*mau-ee*) Second largest of the main Hawaiian islands; 728 square miles in area.

Chapter Four

Haleakala: (*hol-ee-ahk-uh-la*) A dormant volcanic mountain (10,023 feet) on east Maui, located in Haleakala National Park.

Kahoolawe: (*kah-hoe-la-vee*) An island of 45 square miles located about 10 miles southwest of Maui.

Lahaina: (*la-high-na*) A town of 6,100 on the northwest coast of Maui. Once the whaling capital of the mid-Pacific, it's now a center of tourism, shopping and pineapple and sugarcane farming.

Lanai: (*la-nye*) A patio, porch or balcony. Also the name of a small Hawaiian island west of Maui.

Maalaea Bay: (*ma-ah-lay-ah*) The large, open expanse of water on Maui's south shore. The islet of Molokini and the island of Kahoolawe are clearly visible from its shore.

Molokini: (*ma-low-kee-nee*) An islet that's really the tip of an ancient volcano rising from the ocean floor. The U.S. Coast Guard maintains an unmanned beacon light on this uninhabited speck of land.

Monkeypod tree: An ornamental tropical tree that has clusters of flowers, sweet pods eaten by cattle and wood used in carving.

Wailuku: (*wai-loo-koo*) A town of 10,300 in the northwest part of Maui and the Maui County seat; twin city to Kahului (see under chap. 10).

Chapter Five

Kahoolawe: (*kah-hoe-la-vee*) An island of 45 square miles located about 10 miles southwest of Maui.

Lahaina: (*la-high-na*) A town of 6,100 on the northwest coast of Maui. Once the whaling capital of the mid-Pacific, it's now a center of tourism, shopping and pineapple and sugarcane farming.

Lanai: (*la-nye*) A patio, porch or balcony. Also the name of a small Hawaiian island west of Maui.

Maalaea Bay: (*ma-ah-lay-ah*) The large, open expanse of water on Maui's south shore. The islet of Molokini and the island of Kahoolawe are clearly visible from its shore.

Maui: (*mau-ee*) Second largest of the main Hawaiian islands; 728 square miles in area.

Molokini: (*ma-low-kee-nee*) An islet that's really the tip of an ancient volcano rising from the ocean floor. The

U.S. Coast Guard maintains an unmanned beacon light on this uninhabited speck of land.

Oahu: (*ah-wah-hoo*) Hawaii's most populous island and the site of its capital city, Honolulu.

Parasail: (*pair-ah-sail*) A kitelike glider under which a harnessed person rides after being pulled aloft by a powerboat.

Windsurfing: A sport that uses a surfboard with a mast and sail attached. The rider stands upright and leans or moves the mast to steer. Also known as sailboarding.

Chapter Six

Catamaran: (*cat-ah-ma-ran*) A boat with twin hulls side by side.

Haleakala: (*hol-ee-ahk-uh-la*) A dormant volcanic mountain (10,023 feet) on east Maui, located in Haleakala National Park.

Lanai: (*la-nye*) A patio, porch or balcony. Also the name of a small Hawaiian island west of Maui.

Molokini: (*ma-low-kee-nee*) An islet that's really the tip of an ancient volcano rising from the ocean floor. The U.S. Coast Guard maintains an unmanned beacon light on this uninhabited speck of land.

Mynah: (*my-nah*) An Asian starling that's dark brown and black and has a white tail tip and wing markings, with a bright yellow bill and feet.

Chapter Seven

Coconut wireless: Hawaiian slang for what Mainlanders call "the grapevine." People hear things fast in the islands.

Kahoolawe: (*kah-hoe-la-vee*) An island of 45 square miles located about 10 miles southwest of Maui.

Kihei: (*key-hay*) A town of 5,600 on the east side of Maalaea Bay and a growing resort center.

Lahaina: (*la-high-na*) A town of 6,100 on the northwest coast of Maui. Once the whaling capital of the mid-Pacific, it's now a center of tourism, shopping and pineapple and sugarcane farming.

Lanai: (*la-nye*) A patio, porch or balcony. Also the name of a small Hawaiian island west of Maui.

Molokini: (*ma-low-kee-nee*) An islet that's really the tip of an ancient volcano rising from the ocean floor. The U.S. Coast Guard maintains an unmanned beacon light on this uninhabited speck of land.

Ono: (*oh-no*) A large, vigorous mackerel highly prized both as a sport fish and for its excellent flavor. Also known as the wahoo.

Tako: (*tah-koe*) A Japanese word for "octopus" used also in Hawaii.

Zoris: (*zor-eez*) Flat, thonged sandals usually made of straw, leather or rubber.

Chapter Eight

Cover story: A false identity and other details about one's life and work meant to mask the truth.

Kahoolawe: (*kah-hoe-la-vee*) An island of 45 square miles located about 10 miles southwest of Maui.

Lahaina: (*la-high-na*) A town of 6,100 on the northwest coast of Maui. Once the whaling capital of the mid-Pacific, it's now a center of tourism, shopping and pineapple and sugarcane farming.

Lanai: (*la-nye*) A patio, porch or balcony. Also the name of a small Hawaiian island west of Maui.

Safety line: Divers use spools of long, strong line to unwind behind them so they can find their way back when they swim into dangerous places.

Chapter Nine

Auau Channel: (*ah-oo-ah-oo*) The body of water between Maui and the island of Lanai to the west.

Bow: (*bau*) The front part of a boat or ship. Also known as the stem.

Bulkhead: An upright partition separating compartments, as in a ship.

Lava tube: (*lah-vah*) A tube of solid volcanic rock, formed when the outside of a flow of fresh magma, or lava, cools faster than the inside. While the cooler, outside part hardens, the inside lava flows out, leaving a tube. Some tubes are big enough for a man to walk through.

Plankton: Extremely small animal and plant life that

floats or swims weakly in water and is food for many kinds of fish.

Recompression chamber: Commonly but incorrectly called a *de*compression chamber, it "squeezes" a person with air pressure after a dive. That action shrinks any bubbles remaining in the bloodstream so that the crippling, painful and sometimes fatal bends don't strike.

Stalactite: (*stah-lack-tite*) A deposit of material, such as calcium carbonate in a cave, resembling an icicle and hanging from the ceiling or sides of the structure.

Stalagmite: (*stah-lag-mite*) A deposit of material, such as calcium carbonate in a cave, resembling an inverted stalactite and growing up from the floor of the structure.

Chapter Ten

Kahului: (*kah-hoo-loo-ee*) A town of 13,000 on the north shore of Maui; the island's main seaport and site of its only jet airport; twin city to Wailuku.

Maalaea Bay: (*ma-ah-lay-ah*) The large, open expanse of water on Maui's south shore. The islet of Molokini and the island of Kahoolawe are clearly visible from its shore.

Wailuku: (*wai-loo-koo*) A town of 10,300 in the northwest part of Maui and the Maui County seat; twin city to Kahului.

Chapter Eleven

Blackjack: A hand weapon usually made of a leather-wrapped piece of metal with a strap or springy shaft for a handle.

Kiawe: (*kee-ah-vay*) A thorny tree that can grow as tall as a house.

Maui: (*mau-ee*) Second largest of the main Hawaiian islands; 728 square miles in area.

Chapter Thirteen

Kahoolawe: (*kah-hoe-la-vee*) An island of 45 square miles located about 10 miles southwest of Maui.

Lanai: (*la-nye*) A patio, porch or balcony. Also the name of a small Hawaiian island west of Maui.

Maalaea Bay: (*ma-ah-lay-ah*) The large, open expanse of water on Maui's south shore. The islet of Molokini and the island of Kahoolawe are clearly visible from its shore.

Molokini: (*ma-low-kee-nee*) An islet that's really the tip of an ancient volcano rising from the ocean floor. The U.S. Coast Guard maintains an unmanned beacon light on this uninhabited speck of land.

Plumeria: (*ploo-mar-ee-ah*) A shrub or small tree that produces large, fragrant blossoms often used to make leis (flower wreaths or necklaces).

Other Books in the Exciting Ladd Family Adventure Series

Secret of the Shark Pit

A cryptic map leads Josh and his friends on a race with a cruel stranger for priceless Hawaiian treasures. But the hunt turns dangerous when the boys blunder into a shark-filled lagoon.

ISBN 0-929608-14-3

The Legend of Fire

A relaxing vacation on Hawaii's Kona Coast quickly becomes a roller coaster adventure, including Josh's valiant attempt to rescue his kidnapped father from the path of an erupting volcano.

ISBN 0-929608-17-8

Mystery of the Island Jungle

Hawaii's lush jungle island of Kauai soons turns into a maze of terror as Josh and two friends stumble onto a plane wreck and are chased by a screaming, sword-wielding stranger.

ISBN 0-929608-19-4

The Dangerous Canoe Race

Josh and his friends are swept into peril when a bully challenges them to an outrigger canoe race. A swamped boat and a life-threatening storm add to the danger.

ISBN 0-929608-62-3

The Mystery of the Wild Surfer

A mysterious surfer saves Josh from drowning off the coast of Oahu. But when Josh tries to befriend him, Josh finds himself and his family threatened by dangerous men.

ISBN 0-929608-64-X